WHAT BOOKS PRESS

AN IMPRINT OF

THE GLASS TABLE

COLLECTIVE

LOS ANGELES

APRIL, MAY, AND SO ON

FRANÇOIS CAMOIN

Publisher's Cataloging-In-Publication Data

Camoin, François André, 1939-   April, May, and so on / François Camoin.
     p. ; cm.   ISBN-13: 978-0-9823542-4-7   ISBN-10: 0-9823542-4-X
1. Short stories, American. I. Title.

PS3553.A437 A67 2009
813/.54   2009924552

What Books Press
23371 Mulholland Drive, no. 118
Los Angeles, CA 91364

WHATBOOKSPRESS.COM

Cover art: Gronk, *untitled*, mixed media on paper, 2009
Book design by Ashlee Goodwin, Fleuron Press.

APRIL, MAY, AND SO ON

For Shelley.

CONTENTS

SOME KIND OF SWEETNESS

"SO WHY DO THEY CALL you Dancer?" the girl on the barstool next to him wants to know.

Dancer rolls up his right sleeve and shows her the tattoo: Fred Astaire in top hat and tails doing the two-step across Dancer's biceps.

She traces it with a fingernail. Dancer likes the sexy gesture but it makes him feel a little uncomfortable.

"I was drunk in Yokohama one night on shore leave," he says. "There was this little Japanese tattoo guy that liked American movies."

"You were in the Navy?"

"I've seen the world," Dancer says.

The girl looks about eighteen years old, and Dancer feels he's probably doing the wrong thing, but here he is, out of town and out of luck in Port Arthur, Texas. He needs a little company. Just talking couldn't hurt, he tells himself.

"Can you like flex your muscle and make him dance?" the girl says.

"What I had in mind was a plain old American eagle," Dancer says. "I was very traditional when I was a kid. But I sort of passed out in the chair and the guy with the needle had the last word."

"Can you make him dance?" the girl says. "Come on."

"I don't even know your name," Dancer says.

"Eileen."

Dancer makes a fist for her and Fred Astaire actually does move; it's not exactly *An American in Paris*, but it's the best he can do.

"I'm glad you didn't get the eagle," Eileen says.

"I am too," Dancer says. "Now that I've had time to think about it."

"You talk funny," Eileen says. "You don't sound like the people around here."

"I'm from Oregon," Dancer says. "I was hoping to get work in this new refinery they were supposed to put up."

The only thing they're building in Port Arthur now, Dancer found out after he drove nearly three thousand miles down from Portland, is a memorial museum for Janis Joplin. Everybody tells him it's going to be a great thing for this town. Bring tourists from everywhere.

"So now you're broke and you can't go home, right?"

"I'm going home," Dancer says. "I'm just sort of putting it off."

Eileen waves to the bartender for another round. "My treat," she says.

The bartender puts a clean glass in front of Dancer and pours Dos Equis in it too fast; it builds up a big head and Dancer has to wait until the foam dies down before he can drink.

"Doesn't this guy look exactly like Willie Nelson?" Eileen says to the bartender. The kid looks at Dancer and nods. "If you say so."

"I like older men who look kind of sad," she tells Dancer.

"Older than what?" Dancer says.

"Get yourself a headband and a pony tail," she says, "and if you could sing you could go on the road right now."

"I think I need to make a call," Dancer says.

The phone is in back corner of the bar, and while he feeds in quarters and picks out the numbers for home, Dancer watches the girl. She's not exactly pretty, but exactly pretty wouldn't do much for Dancer right now anyway. What he needs is some kind of sweetness.

"You didn't have any luck," his wife says right away when she picks up the phone.

"I'll be coming home," Dancer says.

"I suppose you're in a bar."

"Be reasonable," Dancer says. "Where would you like me to be? The art museum?"

"I'll be looking for you," she says. Her voice doesn't give Dancer a clue how she feels about it, one way or the other.

"It'll be two-three days if the car holds up," Dancer says. "Longer if I've got to stop and fix it someplace along the way."

"You take care now," she says.

He'd like to explain to her that he's not planning to do anything stupid, but that sometimes things just work out in a way you didn't intend. Instead he says "I love you," and hangs up the phone.

When he gets back to the table, Eileen is putting her cigarettes in her purse, counting out change to leave a tip for the bartender.

"We'll take your car," she says. "Mine's in the shop. I ran into a fire hydrant." She giggles. "Sometimes I just don't look where I'm going, you know how it is."

"Jesus," she says when they get to where Dancer's parked. "It's a monster."

"68 Ford," Dancer says. "390 cubic inch V-8." There's comfort in numbers. "Twelve miles to a gallon," he says. "It's like the Arabs never happened, right?"

They drive through streets that are mostly empty. It might be about one in the morning, Dancer thinks, but he's lost track of time. It's hot and the car windows are down. Dancer smells something that could be the sea. Two or three days from now he'll be back home, smelling a different ocean. They're all connected, Dancer thinks, but there's still all the difference in the world.

"There's where the museum's going to be," Eileen says. Dancer looks and sees a hole in the ground with a plywood fence around it. Somebody has written *Janis is lucky she's dead* in blue spray paint along the plywood.

"Turn left now," Eileen says. "If you go slow you can see where I work."

It's called the Supersonic Car Wash; it takes up a whole block in the middle of little grocery stores and fast-food places. The sign is a big rocket poised as if to take off, with red neon exhaust shooting out of the tail.

"I'm the cashier," Eileen says. She looks harmless and helpless huddled in the seat beside him, leaning against the window.

"Turn right down this little street now," she says. Dancer thinks he'd like to stop the car, slide over and kiss her, and then drive on.

"We're home," she says. She's pointing to three stories of stucco; over the door a sign shaped like a shield is lit up by little floodlights: *Open Arms.*

"It's sort of a joke I guess," she says.

They climb up the stairs side by side. She slips a hand into Dancer's back pocket and leaves it there. "You're a nice man," she says.

When they get into her second-floor apartment the first thing she does is pick up a broom and bang on the ceiling with the handle. "Party time," she yells.

"We've got this thing going," she explains to Dancer. "Roberto and Alice are always up for a party. They do the same for me."

"Is that a Texas thing?" Dancer says. "Or just you and Roberto and Alice?"

She gives him a look like he said something stupid. "Life's a little shaky," she says. "Or didn't you find that out yet?" She's getting glasses out of the kitchen cabinet and setting them on the counter. "If you don't prop it up now and then, who's going to do it for you?"

Dancer can hear footsteps coming down the stairs. Somebody's knocking at the door. Eileen stands up on her toes and gives him a quick kiss. "Right?" she says.

"I'm not sure about this," Dancer says.

"So you love your wife," she says. "I could hear you on the phone. Does that mean you don't fool around?"

"Not often," Dancer says.

"I can respect that. Don't worry about it. We'll have our little party and then you can sleep on the couch and be on your way to Oregon in the morning."

There's a big poster of Willie Nelson tacked to the wall, and Eileen makes Dancer stand next to it while she goes to the bedroom to find her Polaroid.

"Wait a minute," she says. "It needs something." She finds a blue bandanna and ties it around Dancer's forehead. "There," she says. She sights through the viewfinder. "You could be twins," she says.

She's playing "Good-hearted Woman" on the stereo. Roberto and Alice are dancing cheek to cheek, shuffling across the hardwood floor, barely moving. For a second Dancer, dazed by drink and by peculiar circumstances, thinks he actually might *be* Willie Nelson. If he could sing. He imagines life on the road, the bus, the groupies, thousands of people listening for his next note. Jesus but life must be good for some people.

He follows Eileen into the kitchen; she's breaking eggs into a pan, adding chili peppers, onions, hamburger. It doesn't smell like anything Dancer's ever tasted before.

"Texas cooking," he says.

"Pass me the big pepper mill there," Eileen says. She grinds away over the pan until the eggs are covered with what looks to Dancer like a scattering of ashes.

"I like your friends," he says.

"Roberto works for the city," she says. "He's a male meter maid. Alice is a female meter maid. They drive around in those little Jeep things and give people tickets all day long. It's a terrible job; everybody gives them a hard time."

"I sold encyclopedias door to door once," Dancer says.

"Same thing," she says. "People set dogs on you, right?"

When the eggs are done they sit in a circle on the living room floor and eat out of big plastic plates. Dancer's first mouthful is like eating fire, but he drowns it with beer and after that it gets easier.

"This man doesn't want to sleep with me," Eileen says. "Can you believe that?"

"How come?" Roberto says. He's bare-chested except for a little leather vest painted over with peace symbols in silver and DayGlo red and green.

"I *want* to," Dancer explains. "I just don't think I should."

"He's married," Eileen says.

Alice slides a hand under Roberto's vest and strokes his chest. Roberto leans over and kisses her ear. Alice is wearing a semi-transparent blouse and no bra. Dancer tries not to stare, but his eyes keep coming back to the breasts pushing up under the thin cloth.

"Poor boy away from home," Eileen says. She takes Dancer's hand and puts it on her leg, holds it there. "It's OK," she says. "Nobody's going to hurt you."

Alice catches Dancer's eye. "Men really have this thing about breasts, don't they?" she says.

"Jesus," Dancer says. "I mean I'm sorry. I didn't intend to be rude."

"Well why not?" she says. "It's harmless."

"Watch out now," Roberto says.

"Here, take a real look," she says. She unbuttons her blouse and holds it open.

"Jesus," Dancer says.

"She's always showing off," Roberto says.

"I don't know why they make such a fuss," Alice says to Eileen.

"Just breasts," Eileen says.

Dancer shakes his head. "No. They're all different. Beautiful." It seems important to him that the women understand what he means.

"Want to dance?" Alice says.

She buttons up her blouse and they dance. Not normally a graceful man, Dancer finds lightness. He's floating above the floor, toes barely touching the hardwood, holding a pretty girl in his arms.

Alice and Roberto have gone home. Dancer and Eileen are sitting side by side on her couch, watching cartoons on the color TV. It's nearly morning and a peculiar steamy light is coming through the window. On the little screen Bugs Bunny is having a conversation with Elmer Fudd. A sign nailed to a tree in the background says: *Rabbit Season Is Open.* Elmer carries a shotgun and wears a hunter's cap.

"This is a real old one," Eileen says. "You can tell by looking at Bugs Bunny's face—see how pointy it is?"

"He looks hungry enough to eat meat," Dancer says.

"You sure you won't go to bed with me?" Eileen says.

"Pretty sure."

"It wouldn't have to be any big thing, you know. Thrashing around, a little touching and a lick or two. Just for fun." She touches his arm. "Give Fred Astaire there something to think about."

Dancer looks out the window. In the steamy light the buildings outside look magical, important.

"Ok, Ok," she says. "I can see you're not going to. Maybe I'm glad."

"I'd really like to," Dancer says.

"So now you go home and look for work in—where was it?"

"Portland, Oregon," Dancer says.

"Only there isn't any work in Portland, Oregon, right?"

"You've got it," Dancer says.

"Did you ever think what it would be like to have a different life?" she says. "I mean if you'd stayed in the Navy or gone to college or whatever?"

"Or I could have been a rock'n roll star," Dancer says.

Two days later, pushing the Ford across the empty spaces of eastern Oregon, Dancer remembers the photograph. He pulls it out of his pocket, props it on the dashboard in front of him. It really is an amazing resemblance. Dancer and Willie Nelson could be twins.

He remembers the lovely and graceful gesture with which Alice opened her blouse for him. It was, he thinks now, a gift. The Ford smells like steam and brake fluid. He has to exercise judgment to keep it between the white lines at these speeds. The brakes are weak, the steering vague, but he's sure it'll get him home. I could have been Willie Nelson, he says out loud. He squints through the windshield and drives on towards the imprecise boundary where sky meets earth, towards the ocean, towards the wife who says she loves him, and who, Dancer is at this moment certain, means exactly that.

LA VIE EN ROSE

DOGS AND CAMELS, GOATS and monkeys—we are all animals. Our words to each other are the seeds that fall on stony ground. Our gestures of affection are like branches tossed around by a summer squall.

The last time I saw Carter he was already running headlong toward the golden wife, the three impeccable children, the lawn so clean, so smooth it would be a temptation to take off your clothes and roll in his dark green perfect grass like a dog, like a monkey. There are princes in America and already in college he was one of them.

"The lawn is covered with leaves like large dead butterflies," his letter says. "I am afraid I have wasted my life."

I like to sit in the attic like this and stare out at the weather. Clouds like little mushrooms speckle a less than perfect sky. A small gimpy wind shuffles the trees. A child's balloon drifts past the window downward into the back yard.

Sometime soon now my wife will come up here and put her arms around me. "*Quand tu me prends dans tes bras,*" she will whisper.

My friend's letter is typed on thick creamy hand-laid paper. "We were not meant to be like this," he says. "We took 17th Century Poets together and you wrote your epic in terza rima. We sat under the windows, do you remember? The radiators hissed and the snow blew against the glass. Bernard Cohen read aloud from 'Litany in Time of Plague'."

"Tu m'dis des mots d'amour," my wife sings softly in my ear.

I have just written: "O my friend, we *were* meant to be like this." Another balloon drifts downward past the window, descending in small arcs, veering in accord with the gimpy wind.

"Black melancholy," I tell Marie while we divide an avocado, share and share alike. Women are hard; women are soft. Before lunch she and I made puppy love on the carpet of the living room; leaves like beautiful dead butterflies flew against the picture window. On the radio Vivaldi repeated himself: tum-ti, tum-ti, tum-ti, tum-ti, while we nipped and tucked at each other with beastly tenderness.

"His poor children," Marie says now. "Is it inherited, this melancholy?"

"His father hanged himself inside a Giant Orange stand outside of Sacramento," I tell her. I have to explain the Giant Orange, the steel segments painted vividly and welded together to make the great spheres set beside the happy highways of California, among the oleanders covered with dust.

She pretends to understand. She picks up a tiny shrimp and puts it on a piece of avocado; she swallows. She sighs. "And you," she says. "Do you think you have wasted your life?"

Shame and vanity are what keep us going. Fear of the father. Desperately wanting to be loved. She wants me to say no.

"We could make love again," she says.

"The boy has his violin lesson at three o'clock," I remind her. "He'll be coming home."

"Do you think we spoil him?" she says.

"We have only one, dearest."

Behind her, through the sliding glass doors, I can see our back yard which has, inexplicably, become filled with balloons. They are all in this year's colors: mauve, puce, charcoal-gray. Piled knee-deep, they heave and moil like moods, tremble uneasily like bad thoughts, make a chorus of tiny penetrating animal squeaks as they rub against each other.

"Oh my ears," Marie says prettily. "You must rake them away soon or what will people think?"

"Let them think what they like."

She picks up a table-knife and raps me sharply across the knuckles. *"Ça ne se fait pas,"* she says.

This is how we met: I was standing in front of a pissoir on the Place des Ternes, contemplating the gloomy church of St. Ferdinand. A graffito was scrawled on the mushroom-colored metal of the pissoir: *A bas le moment Socratique.*

Much later Marie told me that she fell in love with the angle of the back of my neck, which she described as philosophical.

I kissed her.

"It is not like New York here," she said severely.

We were married on the high seas in a touching ceremony. The captain wore a frock coat for the occasion. After the vows he told stories about his days aboard the Murmansk convoys. He danced the polka with Marie, and wept when he showed us photographs of his children.

In New York I took Marie to see the statue up close. She peered at the inscription. "Wretched refuse?" she said. "Who was this person Emma Lazarus?"

I took her to the suburbs and explained America, where we are all foreigners, and live under certain obligations. "Every day we must make a fresh beginning," I said. I showed her the living room with the picture window, and the three and a half bathrooms. I explained patiently the politics of desire, the economy of marriage within which whims and passing fancies are inscribed, a discourse whose capital letters are sometimes dragons, sometimes roses, an impossible alphabet whose way of being is excess and posturing.

I write to my friend. "William Byrd of Virginia, terrified of his father, came back from a trip and learned of the old man's death. Unable to believe his luck, he had the grave opened to see for himself that his father was truly dead."

From the attic window I can see the balloons; they seem to come from everywhere, down out of the sky, falling out of heaven, clogging the streets, rolling irresistibly over fences, burying our little landscape.

"Perhaps," I tell Marie, "we are witnessing the legendary migration of the balloons."

In the afternoon, when the boy comes home from school, before he goes to his violin lesson, I will explain his obligations. We will rake the balloons together; I will show him the sky, where more balloons will appear, endlessly falling, held up for a moment by the flawed wind before they settle on the grass.

Marie will appear in the doorway and strike a revolutionary pose, one fist in the air. "*A bas les mots de tous les jours,*" she will cry, an American at last.

A TENDER HEART

"DO YOU BELIEVE IN ANYTHING?" Sean says to his father.

The three of us are sitting on wooden chairs outside Eddie's General Store, killing a small-town Sunday afternoon.

"Sure I do," Sonny says. He looks surprised. "Naturally. Lots of things. Tell him, Jack."

"He believes in everything," I say. "You just name it."

Sean is the child Sonny had late in life. Nine years old, he is serious and handsome, with his father's brown hair and big intelligent eyes. He speaks to Sonny as if they were the same age; Sonny doesn't seem to mind.

"How about Jesus?" Sean says. "Do you believe in Jesus?"

Sisters is not so much an actual town as an accident of geography, a place in the road, a thin hedge of little houses and stores on either side of the highway. From here I can see right through to open fields. Hundreds of sprinklers are jetting water into the sunlight; behind the fields are more fields, and behind that the mountains bring landscape to a stop that seems perfectly arbitrary, like the period at the end of a long confused sentence.

"I'm not sure about Jesus," Sonny says.

"Well I don't believe in anything." Sean says this as if he has thought about it long and seriously and come to certain conclusions.

The sunlight is falling exactly badly on these little wooden houses that need paint; there's the smell of hot grass and gasoline; the AM radio in Eddie's store is playing the wrong songs. Cars are cruising by on their way to Portland, or headed east toward Bend. Sonny looks at the cars hopefully, as if he supposes one of them might be bringing him a solution for his problems, or maybe he's hoping one will stop and give him a ride so he can escape. He has the face he wears when he's thinking long thoughts about Addie, or about his ex-wife Margo.

"Breaking up is hard to do," he sings along with the radio.

"People who can't sing shouldn't sing," Sean says. He's clearly not intending to be mean; it's an observation, not a judgment. "I'm going back inside," he says.

Sonny reaches for him. "Wait," he says. "I want to explain something." But the kid is already gone.

"Which Jesus is that?" Sonny says to me. "What is all this?"

A car with New York plates rolls by slowly. The windows are closed, the air conditioning on; if Nature has anything to say to the people inside, they don't want to hear it. Through the glass a middle-aged face stares at us for the few seconds it takes the car to pass by. I feel like an actor in somebody else's movie. Maybe this is what Addie means when she says I'm never really *there*. She's Sonny's girlfriend and she doesn't like me much, but we do respect each other.

"It breaks my heart to hear a kid talk like that," Sonny says. He's hanging his head, looking beat up from another night of gloom and frustration in Addie's company. He is also worried about Margo, who remarried a Seattle insurance man, and has her lawyer working on a custody suit.

Addie and Margo. Women make Sonny crazy but he wants love and there is nowhere else in his vocabulary he can find it.

"A kid his age needs his mother," Sonny says. He's staring past the ectoplasmic houses, seeing, but not *really* seeing, the fields and beyond them the mountains and the text of the wonderful empty sky that could tell us something if only we would make the effort to decipher the blankness, which is perhaps, looked at rightly, only the space between two words.

"It might actually be for the best all around if he went," Sonny says. "Only I don't think I could stand it."

Sonny sits with his hands in his lap, looking sadly at the knuckles on his right fist.

"She says I'm incapable of pleasure. I'm not incapable of pleasure."

From Addie's front porch we can see the sun poised to go down behind Black

Butte. It looks like a big orange beachball balanced on a seal's nose, ridiculous but at the same time climactic.

Sonny's knuckles are bloody from beating on Addie's door, which he has been doing, off and on, for about two hours.

"I might not be too bright about some things, Jack, but I'm a human being. With feelings. She has no right to deny that. I've had my pleasures. She knows it, too, so what does she mean with this *incapable* business?"

"Addie's not a patient person," I tell him.

He shakes his head. I would like to help him out but I don't know where to start. He gets up and bangs on the door again, with his left hand this time. A little breeze comes up and blows through the pine woods. The smell it stirs up reminds me of how pleased I am to be living here in this pretty part of Oregon.

Sonny takes a blue bandanna from his back pocket and wraps it tenderly around his knuckles. "Am I behaving like a jackass?" he says.

"I think so."

"I'm talking about life," he says. His eyes look bright and I'm afraid he might cry. He puts his ear to the door and listens. All he hears is silence; if Addie is in there, she isn't about to give him the satisfaction.

Sonny is for the most part a straightforward man, who never talks about himself in the third person or does any of the other things that indicate weakness or a feminine or devious nature. He has a good and tender heart that has not been coarsened by the psychopathology of everyday life, by the disappointments and betrayals, by the petty triumphs that others enjoy over us.

"Life is all right," I tell him. "Love too. Breaking your knuckles on Addie's door because she won't come out and talk with you is more like something else."

"Don't you think I know that?" he says.

"It's time to go home."

He shakes his head. "I'm not giving up."

I say "Good night, Sonny," and start to leave. Before I can go down the three steps to the street I hear the door open behind me. When I turn there is Addie, leaning out at Sonny, looking displeased. She is a fearsome woman today, all eye-makeup and wide shoulders and electric hair—beautiful, but in that special way that lets you know there will be a high price to pay for any fun you might have together. Sonny ducks past her and goes inside without looking at me.

She gives me a hard stare. "I blame you, Jack," she says.

"I don't encourage him."

"In a thousand little ways," she says.

"Name one."

"Don't play the innocent with me, Jack," she says.

Addie's ex-husband is in town and we all drive to Bend for dinner. We sit by a glass wall where we can look out at the Douglas fir, the grass, a lake with ducks and other waterfowl sporting in the sun. Richard is a shadowy man from Los Angeles, a dealer in hard to obtain commodities. Addie reaches across the table and fingers the nugget of raw gold her ex-husband wears on his chest, hanging from a leather thong. From where I sit the gesture looks almost like love.

"Now *there* is real class," she says.

Richard is undisturbed by hostility. "Once a bitch, always a bitch," he says to Sonny.

"We came here to have a good time," Sonny says.

A swan cruises by on the little lake, his neck bent into the traditional question mark. On the far side of the pond women in bright clothes are playing golf. We're too far away to see the flight of the balls, and it looks from here as if they were engaged in some abstract beautiful exercise with no point outside of gracefulness.

"You're a nothing," Addie says to Richard. She pokes him in the chest. "Nobody will ever get the best of me, but especially not you."

"I'm a romantic person," Sonny explains, though nobody asked him.

Addie goes on staring at her ex-husband. A few seconds go by before she seems to hear Sonny. "What's that supposed to mean?" she says.

Sonny just looks at the swan, which is coming back the other way, trailing a long ripple in the water.

"Well?" Addie says.

"We're all doing the best we can," I tell her.

"Explain that to me," she says. "Tell me how you're doing your best, Jack."

We eat oysters off the shell, which are like an ache of sorts at the back of the throat; they have, not so much *taste* as a feel like something previous to taste. We eat poached salmon and little spring carrots no bigger than the first joint of my forefinger.

"Do you ever forget things you have done?" I say to Addie.

She thinks about it for the time it takes her to stab a carrot with her fork and swallow it. "When are you going to get your own place, Jack?" she says. "They share a house," she explains to Richard. "It's not healthy."

"You know what happiness is?" Sonny says. We all look at him. "Happiness is never wanting anything you can't get at the 7-11."

"That's the stupidest thing I ever heard," Addie says. "Is that one of your ideas, Jack?"

"Don't blame me," I tell her.

"I do," she says. "For a lot of things."

"You seem like a good bunch of people," Richard says. He has a monkey's face, like many people in Los Angeles, wrinkled and tanned, framed by unnaturally black hair.

"I wouldn't want you to think it's always like this," Addie says to her ex-husband. "Usually those two are a little smarter, especially Jack. He's not a good person, but he's not dumb."

After dinner the two of them go off in Richard's Eldorado Cadillac, with the top folded down and Addie sitting up high on the back of the front seat, like a pretty cheerleader or a girl with a poor reputation.

I hand Sonny a beer and sit down with him on the couch. "Isn't it sad how people get old?" he says.

"You and me?"

"Everybody," he says.

We've been watching an old black and white movie on the TV, with Eddie Albert and Randolph Scott in the Air Force. Eddie Albert looks about eighteen years old here, full of bounce and vitality.

Sonny disappears for a minute to check on Sean, who is asleep in the back bedroom. Through the open door I can see the two posters over the kid's bed. One's a still from *Casablanca*—Bogart at a table, a drink in front of him, a cigarette hanging from his lip. The other is a stylized Jim Morrison speckled with tiny black and white flowers. Of the two, it's Bogart that looks like the innocent.

"He's all right," Sonny says.

"Of course he's all right."

"Margo thought I was crazy," Sonny says. "When he was first born I used to get up sometimes two or three times in the night to make sure he was still breathing."

On the TV Eddie Albert is bent over a bombsight, dropping them straight, his mind bent on achieving purity of form. Beneath the plane unrolls sand, the desert, the hard truth.

"Would you like to watch something else?"

"Do you think they're sleeping together?" he says.

"Addie and Richard?"

"I couldn't stand it," he says.

"What do you expect out of life?"

"Yes, but Jesus!" he says.

"They deserve each other."

"Maybe," he says.

Later he comes into my room and wakes me up. I'm having a complicated dream where I'm dancing with a dog who speaks like my father. When I open my eyes Sonny is sitting by the bed holding a letter in his hand.

"It came today but I didn't show it to you," he says.

The letter is from Margo's lawyer, a man named Cantor. It says Sonny can either give up the kid voluntarily or Margo will go to court and take him anyway.

"Can they do that?" Sonny says.

I'm still half in my dream, waltzing the black dog across a hardwood floor to the music of Guy Lombardo. The dog is on his hind legs, his paws on my shoulders. From the beast's mouth my father speaks. "Be a better person," he says.

"Yes," I tell Sonny. "They can."

"No," Sonny says.

I'm thinking *why a dog*.

"No they can't," Sonny says. "Not in this world."

———

Sonny sits with me in Addie's living room. His head hangs down; he draws little circles on the coffee table with his thumb. He looks like an old man. We got the bad news in the mail today. Sonny's ex-wife, the insurance man, and the lawyer named Cantor charmed the judge with the music of family, stability, convention, the melody of the middle life.

"He has to go back next week," Sonny says.

The weather has turned nasty, the way it does sometimes in this part of the country in late spring. A high wind from out of nowhere rattles the trees outside. Wet snow spatters on Addie's insulated glass.

Sean is in the kitchen making a milkshake. I wander in there and ask him what he thinks of all this. He shrugs, looks down at his shoes, makes circles on the counter with his thumb.

"I wouldn't mind living with Margo," he says. "She's OK, sort of. But I'm pretty sorry for my dad."

"He can handle it." I'm trying to make the kid feel better.

"I'm not so sure," Sean says. "Sonny likes me a lot."

"What are you going to do?"

"What am I *supposed* to do?"

"I don't know," I tell him.

"I'm just a kid," he says.

I follow him back into the living room. Addie is standing over Sonny, who is still slumped on the couch.

"Get on a plane," she says. "Leave town and take Sean to New Mexico or Arkansas or someplace. They'll never find you."

"I don't know," Sonny says.

"I suppose you're thinking about you and me," Addie says. "Well don't. Richard wants me back and I'm going. So you might as well get out of town, go somewhere and make yourself a life with the kid."

"I don't think it would be such a good idea," Sonny says.

"It's what *I'm* doing," Addie says. She looks at me. "Don't encourage him," she says.

"This is terrible," Sonny says.

"Richard's not all that bad. Life with him was interesting if it wasn't anything else." She dips a finger in Sean's milkshake and sucks off the foam, does a little pirouette past the coffee table, looks out at the snow. "God how I have hated living in the country," she says.

"Oregon's just a place," Sonny says. "This Richard business isn't rational."

Addie looks at me. "Don't say one word," she says.

"This is all going wrong," Sonny says.

"I blame you, Jack," Addie says.

She means she blames me for what Sonny's thinking, not for the things that happened, which nobody could have helped. She rises out of her chair. Her index finger shoots out to impale me on the point of hard truth.

"I blame—" she starts to say. But Sonny stands up and puts a finger on her lips.

"Do something," Sean says. He's talking to me.

Before I can, there's a knock on the door.

"Who could that be?" Addie says.

"We're all here," Sonny says. He looks puzzled.

I open the door. A man and a woman are standing on the porch. They're holding hands. Behind them a Hertz Plymouth is nosed half-way into the ditch. The woman looks a little bit like Addie, especially around the eyes.

"What kind of a place is this?" the woman says. "This weather is just simply ridiculous."

"Jesus," Sonny says.

"I thought I'd find you here," the woman says. She's looking at Sonny.

"Margo," Sonny says.

"We've come to get Sean," she says.

The man holds his hand out to me. He looks embarrassed; it's clear this isn't his idea of a good time. "I was hoping we could do all this in a friendly manner," he says.

Margo takes Sean by the arm and starts to pull him across the living room. Sonny lets go of Addie and takes the kid's other arm. They tug back and forth for a while. Sean's crying, big tears rolling down his face, but he's not saying anything.

"You shouldn't be doing that," Margo's new husband says.

"Stay out of it," Margo tells him.

"Get her out of my house," Addie says to Sonny.

"Do you see what you're doing to this child?" Margo says.

It takes about half an hour but finally everybody gets calmed down. Addie makes a pot of coffee and we sit in her living room, trying not to look at each other. The insurance man stirs his coffee with his index finger; across the room Sonny sits with his head in his hands.

"So we came a few days early," Margo says finally. "So what's the big deal here. I mean I've got a court order. I'm entitled."

Nobody says anything for a while. It's like there's a question hanging in the air here, that nobody has an answer for. I'm thinking about my dream where my father was a dog. Why a dog? I remember reading that the unconscious is structured like a language, but a dog?

"Do you believe in anything?" Sean says. He's looking at Margo.

"We can give you a good home," the insurance man says. He licks the coffee off his finger and looks embarrassed, obviously thinking he said the wrong thing.

"I wasn't talking to you," Sean says.

"Don't be rude to your father," Margo says.

"In Jesus," Sean says. "Do you believe in Jesus?"

"What have you been teaching this child?" Margo says.

Sonny stands up and walks to the middle of the room. "Stop, please, everybody. I'm asking you," he says. "This is what will happen. Addie will go back with Richard and have a life. I don't think it's going to be a good one, but it's her life, isn't it? Sean will go live with Margo and have a new father and come back every summer to see me."

"What kind of a father is he going to have," Addie says. "An insurance man?"

"Well," Sonny says, "I guess I can't do very much about that."

"If you were half a man," Addie says.

"Does anybody believe in anything?" Sean says.

"I blame you, Jack," Addie says.

LOOKING FOR STRANGE

EVERYTHING OUT THERE looks perfectly ordinary today. White stucco walls. Your normal blue sky. Palm trees. The lawn sprinklers. It's a David Hockney painting of the good life. The light from above hints at doom, but that's in the future, nothing definite. I'm standing by the sliding glass door, watching Ed and Rita play gin rummy on a little round metal table by the pool. Ed's a retired aeronautical engineer; he and Rita manage the complex. There's not a whole lot for them to do—the owner has a pool man, a gardener, clean-up crews to paint the apartments when somebody moves out. Ed and Rita collect the rents; they talk to the tenants; Ed fixes things.

Marge and Shelley are churning up the blue water, swimming laps. They are both dark-haired, athletic, confident. I watch them do a racing turn together and come back the other way. They share the apartment below mine. At night they play their music on the stereo: Rolling Stones, Blood Sweat and Tears, Jefferson Airplane. They play it loud; I could call Ed and have him talk to them, but actually I like the music. The shorter one is Marge; the other is Shelley.

The phone rings; I reach out to pick it up without taking my eyes off the swimmers.

"Yeah?"

"What kind of a way to answer the phone is that? Are you depressed or something?" my sister says.

"Hi Peggy," I say.

I'm not depressed, exactly. It's more that the inside of my head feels like a desert. Little animals running around looking for shade. Broken bottles going violet in the sun. Plants that look like minerals. A place where you might not want to live.

"Your voice is funny," she says.

"Everything's all right, I swear."

"It's not," she says. "I know you, Jack." I can feel her pulling herself together for my sake on the other end of the phone. "Take a deep breath," she says. "Count to ten, then we'll talk."

"I'm perfectly calm," I say.

"Are you in love again?" she says.

"I don't think so."

"Every time you fall in love you get a little weird," my sister says. "You do things you wouldn't do otherwise."

The women have finished their laps and are helping each other dry off with big fluffy yellow towels. Marge waves at me and I slide open the door to hear what she's saying.

"You going to come out and swim later?"

"Maybe," I say.

"Who were you talking to?" Peggy says.

"One of the girls by the pool wanted me to come out and swim."

"Which one?"

"Marge."

"I think they're lesbians," my sister says.

"They just want me to swim, that's all," I say.

I watch Marge and Shelley rubbing suntan oil on each other. They're nice girls. If they're lesbians it's not their fault.

"I'm getting married next month," Peggy says.

"You and Bob?"

"*Rob*," she says. "*Rob*. His name is *Rob*. You never get it right. It's because you don't like him."

"He reminds me of a kid I knew in grade school who used to do perverse things in class."

"What kind of things?" Peggy's always on the lookout for strange. It's like a hobby. She calls me on the phone at work sometimes, and reads me articles from the National Enquirer.

"Under his desk," I say. "You want details?"

"I think we'll go to Tahiti for the honeymoon," she says. She likes detail, but not if it has to do with sex. Whenever she hears something sexual coming up in conversation, she veers away.

"Romantic," I say. I try to imagine my sister and Rob in Tahiti. I can't visualize him in Bermuda shorts and a sun hat among the bare-breasted native girls. I can't imagine Peggy married to such a man.

"Are you sure about this?" I say.

"I know you think he's peculiar but I love him," she says. "Besides, what else am I going to do? You think my life's a joke? Ha, ha, ha, I'm dying here."

In the Ralph's Supermarket on Topanga Canyon Boulevard I look for a big fluffy yellow towel like the ones Marge and Shelley were using.

"Sort of a chrome-yellow," I say to the clerk. I can tell she's not very interested.

"You don't see it, we don't have it," she says. "How about this?" She holds up an orange beach towel, much too small.

"Has to be yellow," I say.

"It's not the color that gets you dry," she says.

"You sound sort of cranky today," I say. "Is something the matter?"

"Don't be personal," she says. "I don't allow customers to get personal with me."

I apologize and offer to buy her a cup of coffee. She says yes after thinking about it for a minute. We go and sit down in the little cafeteria at the back of the store.

"It's a just this dumb job," she says. "I hate, you know, helping people." She puts a cigarette in her mouth and leans forward for me to light it. She takes a couple of deep drags, then turns the cigarette around and inspects the end to make sure it's burning evenly.

"Men always do that," she says.

"Do what?"

"Pull the match away too quick. They never want to wait that extra second. It's not as if you had anything you'd rather do," she says.

Her nametag says Bobby-Jo. She reminds me of the figure-skaters I've been watching on television. Very attractive, lots of essential vitality, but a little bit detached, impersonal, as if this was a performance. As if she wasn't *there*, exactly.

"I don't really do this," she says, waving her cigarette at the supermarket behind us. "I'm a writer. I'm already very good. Tony Bill's reading one of my screenplays right now. Maybe he'll buy it. It's a sort of Stirling Silliphant thing—comedy, but with a lot of tenderness."

———

I meet Peggy at the Yellowfingers restaurant on Ventura Boulevard. I'm supposed to be at work, but she said on the phone it was an emergency. I told Detweiler I needed some personal time. "You're not irreplaceable," he said. "Go ahead. You going to be back this afternoon?"

"Maybe," I said.

"Maybe I won't fire you," he said.

Detweiler's not a bad person; he just likes to make his needs known. He's about five feet tall and I think he had a bad childhood. I'm explaining all this to Peggy in the restaurant because I'm not ready to talk about her problem yet. She's drinking some kind of pink fizzy liquid through a straw and waiting for me to get done.

"Detweiler's gay," I tell her.

"Probably not," my sister says. "You have no instinct for these things at all. I could tell about Marge and Shelley the first time I saw them."

She sucks up more of her pink drink through the straw and makes a face. She's been crying. The makeup covers it up pretty well, but her eyes are red.

"So what's the problem?"

"Rob called me up last night and pretended he was somebody else. He said he'd seen me at work and would I go out with him. He put on this English accent and made his voice sound real deep, but I knew."

The waiter is a young kid with bleached hair. He starts to recite the specials for the day but Peggy cuts him off. "Snails," she says. "I'm in the mood for snails."

"Why would Rob do a thing like that?" I ask her after the kid leaves.

"Anyhow that's not the worst part," Peggy says.

"Take a deep breath," I tell her. "Count to ten. It'll be all right."

"No it won't," she says.

I turn my head to look at the simple sequence of traffic going by on Ventura Boulevard. One car then the next car. Different colors. Animal shapes. Nothing to worry about.

"I thought I'd teach him a lesson and I said yes, I'd go to dinner."

"And?"

"Rob came over to my apartment and started yelling at me," Peggy says. She stabs a snail and yanks it out of the shell with the little fork. She holds it up to the light to look at it. "Ugly little thing," she says. "But they taste so good." She sucks if off the fork into her mouth.

"He was like a crazy person," she says. "He wouldn't admit it was really him on the phone."

"So how did he explain that he knew about your date?"

"He broke my coffee table and some dishes," Peggy says, not answering my question. "He called me terrible names."

I wake up in bed in Bobby-Jo's apartment. She's sleeping on her stomach, her face buried in the pillow, one arm draped across me. On the floor beside the bed is her screenplay which I was reading last night. It's not bad—comedy, a little tenderness. The people in the story seem to like each other. They lead interesting lives.

She lifts her head, opens one eye. Without make-up she looks fragile, younger than she did in the store, more like a real person.

"I despise casual sex," she says.

I wait for her to say something else. To tell me if she thinks what we did is casual sex. If she's mad at me. If she's happy we slept together. She jumps out of bed and walks off.

"Coffee in five minutes," she says over her shoulder. "Meet me in the kitchen."

I wait for the bathroom, brush my teeth with some of Bobby-Jo's toothpaste and the tip of my finger, look in the mirror. It's me, all right, a little older than I remembered, but not looking too bad.

In the kitchen we sit across the table from each other. My coffee-mug has a big red heart on it. Hers has cartoon elephants making elephant love.

"You like pop-tarts?" she says. "I've got strawberry or apple. Or I've got some English muffins. I don't have any eggs."

"Just coffee's fine."

"This is sort of embarrassing," she says. "This morning-after stuff. If you'd like to leave you don't have to be polite."

I walk around the table and kiss her. We go back to the bedroom. She doesn't make a big production out of it, but it's fun.

Peggy calls while I'm watching *LA Law* on the television. "Girl Gives Birth to Bigfoot's Baby," she says.

Downstairs the girls are playing the Doors. *Riders of the Storm.* Every once in a while, when Jim Morrison stops singing, I think I can hear a little whimper, a moan. I'd like to think they're making love on the living room floor down there while they listen to the music. Does that make me a bad person?

"Rob's coming over to dinner tomorrow night," she says. "I want you to come too."

"I don't think so."

"No," she says. "I mean if he's really crazy I shouldn't be marrying him, right? I need an outside opinion."

"Can I bring somebody?"

"I knew it," she says. "You *are* in love. I could tell when we talked on the phone the other day."

"I hadn't even met her yet."

"You were going to," she says.

After she hangs up I try to read for a while, but I can't concentrate, so I go down to the pool. Marge and Shelley are just coming out of their place. Rita and Ed are playing cards.

"Haven't seen you down here in a long time, Jack," Marge says.

"We missed you," Shelley says. She gives me a hug. She's a big girl and we almost stumble into the water.

"Whoops!" she says.

"I thought he was better balanced than that," Marge says.

They spread a big green beach towel open on the cement; I lie down between them. I'm wearing my gray suit; they've got on string bikinis. I stare up past the apartment roofs at the ordinary blue sky and the tops of the palm trees. I'm glad I live here.

"I should go get my camera," Rita says.

"You look so hot," Shelley says. "Why don't you go up and put on your bathing suit."

"We could have a swim together," Marge says.

"He might drown," Shelley says. "He's not too coordinated."

"We'll save him," Marge says. "Give him a little CPR if he looks like he needs it."

Peggy answers the phone. Rob was supposed to be here half an hour ago;
we've been making conversation and eating Gouda cheese and little Danish
crackers, drinking white wine. Being polite with each other. When we first
got here Peggy and Bobby-Jo went into the kitchen and stayed there for about
ten minutes; I could hear them whispering. Every once in a while one of them
would pop her head around the door and give me a raised eyebrow.

"Who's this?" Peggy says into the phone.

"Is that right?" she says. She makes frantic waving motions which mean I
should go into the bedroom and pick up the extension.

A man's voice says "You have a face like a fourteenth-century painting."

The voice is artificially resonant, like somebody speaking through a cardboard
tube. It has a stagey English accent.

"Do you believe in love at first sight?" the voice says.

"You're a sick person," Peggy says.

"I beg your pardon?" the voice says.

I sit there for a minute on the edge of her bed after she slams the phone down.
Her room has pink curtains, the bedspread is full of little flowers, the wallpaper is
an endless repetition of koala bears. I think about doom. The sadness of everyday
life.

When I go back to the living room the two women are sitting on the couch.
Bobby-Jo's got her arms around Peggy.

"Go on home," Bobby-Jo says to me. "I'll take care of things."

There's a golf tournament on the TV, but I'm not really paying attention.
Marge and Shelley are taking turns making fancy dives off the board. They've
traded in their string bikinis for black Speedo suits and they look serious,
muscular. Shelley does a running forward flip, misses her timing and hits
the water on her back. I wait for a second; I'm afraid she's hurt herself,
but she comes up laughing. On the TV somebody who looks vaguely like
Arnold Palmer lines up a long putt. The ball dipsy-doodles its way down the
green, runs around the lip, slides about six feet past the cup. There's a long
disappointed "Oooh!" from the crowd.

Later I wander outside to the pool. The girls have gone inside, but Ed and Rita are still out there playing gin rummy. A little wind has come up and Ed's using a can of RC Cola to hold down the discards. In the pool I try lying on my back, but my feet sink and pretty soon I'm floating vertically with only my eyes above the water, like a hundred and sixty pound frog. It feels pleasant and I stay there, holding my breath as long as I can, watching Ed and Rita turn the cards. They've been married a long time but I can see they still like each other. The weird light says doom but it's been singing the same predictable tune for years and nothing's happened. It's probably going to be OK for a while yet.

THE NATURAL CONDITION
OF THE WORLD

IT'S RAINING AND THE WIPERS are slapping back and forth in front of the movie. *God*, Asher thinks, *I love times like this*. Up against the sky several cheerleaders are prancing across the screen, flashing their tight little asses, waving red and yellow pom-poms.

"Cheap sex and horror—you can't beat that on a Friday night," Asher says.

Everything out there is rainy and damp, but inside Asher's 1961 Cadillac with the powder-blue leather seats and the good heater, it's all cozy and comfortable. If he looks out the side windows Asher can see old fat cars washed by the rain, squatting in the gravel, full of people not exactly like himself, but close enough

It's the last drive-in in Salt Lake City, which was once maybe the drive-in movie capital of the world. Next spring this one will be gone too. The signs are already up: *Home of the New World Plaza*. The bulldozers are waiting to roll up the gravel bumps and tear out the speaker posts and dig the foundations for Osco Drugs and Ace Hardware and New Age Videos, all those little places where Asher goes on Saturday mornings to buy the things he thinks he can't do without.

On the screen a teen-age halfback wriggles through the opposition to score a touchdown. The cheerleaders make a pyramid of young hard bodies to celebrate.

"Don't you love this?" Asher says.

"It's America," Barbara says.

Last week Asher took her to see *Texas Chainsaw Massacre* and she thought *that* was America. Barbara is a high-powered woman, a radio executive with a BMW and a condominium in Governor's Plaza. She is trying to educate Asher and make him a better person. So far it hasn't worked. Asher doesn't think he needs educating. He went to college and read some books. If he's engaged in ignorance, it's voluntary. He works in the sheet-metal shop because other occupations seem too complicated. He's after simplicity, but it's getting away from him all the time.

"It's just a drive-in movie," he says. He reaches down for the switch and tilts the big seat back so they can be more comfortable. Barbara puts her head on his shoulder and they sit like this, watching the screen and listening to the crackly dialogue from the speaker hung in the window.

The premise of this movie is that after every game the cheerleaders in this little Texas town near the Big Thicket choose one of the football players and take him out somewhere dark and quiet. He thinks he's going to get some cheap sex, but instead they tie him up, dance around him, cut off his head with a cleaver.

"Female rage," Barbara says, watching the blood fly. The girls put the dead boy's head on a stick and dance around with it. Barbara laughs but when Asher looks at her a second later she is crying.

"It's just sex and violence. Nothing to be worried about. Been going on for a long time."

"Not where I live," she says.

Six months ago Asher's wife Cindy walked out on him, leaving the sleeper couch, the color TV, and the dog which Asher never got along with in the first place. "You might have been my high-school sweetheart," she stuck her head back in the door to say, "but you're also a peculiar person and I don't love you any more."

Asher almost said "You're breaking my heart and I'll never love anyone else," but a sense of what was proper stopped him. By the time he got beyond proper and opened his mouth to tell her about love, Cindy had slammed the door and was gone out of his life.

Stella, the dog, pees in the corners of the apartment. When Asher swats her with a rolled-up newspaper to teach her better manners, she snarls and snaps at his hand. Asher buys her favorite dog food, takes her for walks in the park, tries to deal with this problem like a civilized person, but it isn't working out.

The movie is sequential, a canny Hollywood narrative, the scenes logically connected. Blood and dancing in the woods; the fat coach in his office tearing out his hair, wondering why his best players are disappearing one by one; young love in the back seat of Buicks; more dancing, more blood.

"I do love this," Asher says. "I can't help it."

Barbara lifts her head from his shoulder and looks at him seriously. "You're an intelligent person," she says. She isn't crying any more but the tears have left traces that Asher finds endearing.

Asher suspects she's right. He is an intelligent person. But then what? Is intelligence what it's all about?

Since Cindy left Asher has a recurring dream where he's in bed with two women—they are naked, gentle, full of invention and kindness. When he wakes up he is disappointed because he knows that it's unlikely such a thing is ever going to happen to him in this life.

"If you'd only pay attention," Barbara says. "To me, I mean. I could teach you things."

Asher lights a cigarette and rolls down the window a couple of inches to let the smoke out. A little rain comes in, blown by the wind; it feels good. Barbara doesn't like for him to smoke, but Asher can't seem to give it up—doesn't want to, to tell the truth. For Asher, the cigarette is a little place where he can go any time and be alone. Like magic, he can strike a match and be gone. Away from himself, too, that's the beauty and the wonder of it.

"Sometimes I think you actually take these movies seriously," Barbara says.

"I do."

"Don't kid me," Barbara says. She moves closer to Asher, takes his hand and puts it on her breast.

This is supposed to feel good, Asher tells himself.

Asher would like to love the dog, but Stella still pees in the corners and the apartment is beginning to smell bad. "Sooner or later we're going to have to stop this," he tells her. The dog climbs up beside him and goes to sleep. She's a big dog, half black Lab, half something else, and she takes up most of the couch, so that Asher has to make himself small. "I mean it," he says. "We can't go on living like this."

When Barbara calls he's watching *The NFL Today*. Jimmy the Greek and

Brent Musburger are talking about cancer. Asher slept through part of the beginning and isn't certain how they got on the subject. While he slept Stella put her head on his leg and drooled on his pants. "Jesus," he says.

"Who are you talking to?"

"The dog," Asher says.

"It isn't healthy for you to be alone all the time."

"I'm not alone," Asher says.

"She doesn't even like you."

"What is it you wanted?" Asher says.

"Let's go somewhere."

It's a notion Barbara has now and then, that they should get into Asher's Cadillac and just drive. They saw *Badlands* at the drive-in and Barbara fell in love with Martin Sheen bumping his stolen car across the endless spaces of Nebraska with Cissy Spacek beside him. Murderers, sure, but at the same time sweet kids.

While he listens to today's version of Barbara's road fantasy Asher looks around his apartment. Entropy. He's been reading Henry Adams and thinking about the heat-death of the universe. What we've got here, he says to himself, is entropy in little—dust that falls seemingly from nowhere on everything he owns, cracks in the plaster, books whose pages are turning yellow and fragile, everything returning slowly to a primordial and undifferentiated state which, Asher suspects, is the natural condition of the world.

What Asher used to like best about Cindy was the way she could never be still. What he didn't like was the way he was always seeing himself through her eyes— Asher carrying the groceries, Asher sprawled on the couch watching the NFL, Asher making love. It was all, viewed like that, faintly ridiculous. It distorted his sense of the present, put him always a fraction of a second behind himself.

In Pay 'N Pak this morning, thinking back on his married life, he stumbles into the bathroom fixtures department, finds himself in front of a triple mirror, doesn't recognize the person staring back at him. The man in the mirror scratches his nose and Asher thinks *what a curious coincidence*, until the synapses reorganize themselves and it comes to him that this is Asher he's staring at. I look like hell, he tells himself. I need a haircut. I need to lose thirty pounds. I need to get hold of my life. But this life he wants to get hold of is slippery and elusive, and Asher suspects he's not about to get much of a grip on it no matter how hard he tries.

Asher wanders the aisles, bumping into ordinary people who probably ought to get hold of themselves too. He's forgotten why he came here. To buy something, sure, but what? He looks at desk-lamps, considers step-ladders. Paint-guns that look like weapons from Star Trek. Kerosene heaters. Answering machines. Programmable thermostats. There's a certain fascination in *things*.

Asher thinks of the people who invented all these objects cunningly displayed to tempt him. He pushes the buttons on an electric range: *High, Medium, Simmer*. Why not *Low*, he wonders. A quick motion half-glimpsed makes him look up, overcome with an unbearable sense of the familiar. Half the length of the aisle away from him, looking at kitchen cabinets, is Cindy. She turns and sees him. Immediately Asher feels like a fool. A middle-aged man in Pay 'N Pak on a Saturday morning.

"Hey," Asher says.

"It's you," Cindy says. She looks about the same as the day she told him she didn't love him any more. Prettier maybe. If she's been sad, it doesn't show.

"Want to get some coffee?" Asher says.

"Why?" she says.

"Let's be civilized," Asher says.

Asher hates the little tin metal ashtrays that skitter around the table when you try to put out your cigarette. They were designed to make you feel bad about smoking. Across the table from him, Cindy looks like the girl he used to fumble around with in the back of his father's Chevrolet when they were fifteen years old. It's an illusion, Asher knows that, but here in the Bagel Nosh, with the smell of pastrami and pickles, the Formica table and the terrible ashtrays, she still looks like a cheerleader.

We've got a history, he'd like to say, but this girl sitting across from him is too young to have a history, so Asher shuts his mouth and reaches for another smoke.

"Go ahead, kill yourself," Cindy says. "Only don't think I care, because I don't."

"You seeing anybody?" Asher says. He thought he'd caught a glimpse of her once, about a month back, riding down South Temple with a businessman-looking guy in a Mercedes 190. When they pulled ahead Asher saw the license plate: EGO.

"You and Barbara living together yet?" Cindy says.

For a second Asher wants to lie, wants to make up an elaborate story in which he's found happiness. But it won't wash; Cindy knows him too well.

"Nope," he says. "Just me and the dog."

"I can't help it if you don't like the dog," Cindy says.

"It's sort of a Mexican standoff, the two of us," Asher says. "Why don't you take her—I could bring her over to your place tonight if you want."

Cindy shakes her head. It's one of her quick gestures that leave no room for argument or compromise. She actually *doesn't* look near as old as me, Asher thinks. "Are you happy now?" he says.

"I don't think I ever did love you," Cindy says. "Not really."

———

Out in his driveway Asher is waxing the Cadillac. The paint is thin on the top of the trunk and on the hood, where the sun and the rain have bleached the blue almost white. Like an old bone, Asher thinks, rubbing in the wax. He has enough money to have it repainted, but not to have it done well, so he's decided to let it go for a while. Besides it looks OK in its own way now. Barbara is sitting in a chaise lounge on the grass, sipping a beer, watching him work. Every now and then she absent-mindedly pats Stella on the head. The dog looks happier with her than it ever does with Asher.

"You love that damn car more than you do me," Barbara says.

Asher thinks about that for a minute. He can't say for sure if she's kidding or not. "That's America," he says.

"I'm serious," she says.

"I've had her a long time now." He's working on the hubcaps with the chrome polish. It's magical the way the little specks of rust disappear under the cloth, as if they'd been illusions in the first place.

"Why don't we get married," Barbara says.

Asher works on the bumper, careful not to put chrome polish on the rubber strips where it will leave a white film when it dries. "I don't think we'd better," he says.

"You know what happens to people like you? They end up all alone in a hotel room when they're seventy years old, with pee stains on their underwear."

Asher stops polishing. It feels like a curse. If he knew how, he'd make the sign to ward off the evil eye.

"You'll scrape together your pennies once a day and go out to go buy Twinkies at the 7-11," Barbara says.

Asher sits on the ground and leans back against his car; he senses a terrible truth here.

"I could save you from all that," she says.

Asher doesn't say anything. His eyes are closed; a little film inside his head shows him to himself: aged, unshaven, wearing pants that bag at the seat, alone. On the other hand it might not be so bad.

"Or else you could go back to Cindy," Barbara says.

"She wouldn't have me."

"I never said she was dumb," Barbara says.

———

At the sheet-metal shop the next day, Asher takes a break and calls Cindy from the pay phone. All morning long he's been bending thin steel sheets to make truck toolboxes, feeding the metal into the machine, which makes precise Euclidean corners, turning two dimensions into three. The work is both dumb and delicate—a couple of Asher's friends at the shop sport three-fingered hands because they let their minds wander at the wrong instant.

He drops the quarter in the slot and waits for Cindy to answer. When she does, he forgets for a second why he called.

"What do you want?" she says.

Asher remembers what he decided this morning. "I'm coming over tonight and bringing the dog."

"No you're not," she says.

"She likes you, she doesn't like me," Asher says. "I don't see what's so difficult about that."

"You wouldn't," Cindy says.

Back at his machine, feeding in the long metal sheets, Asher thinks *well I did it again*. He'd like his life to make sense, but it's clear that it isn't going to, anyway not in the near future. He hasn't, if he stops to think about it, got any more of a grip on himself than most of the people he knows. And that isn't nearly enough.

At lunch he sits with Amos, who's been working there for nine years and still has all his fingers except for the first joint on the index finger on the left hand.

"You got to have a good car," Amos says. "The rest don't matter a bit." He wears what looks like a tiny sock, cut from one finger of a cotton glove, over the stump of his index. Asher doesn't know if it's a sign of a delicate nature, not wanting to subject others to the sight of his mutilation, or if it's just to protect himself. Back in college Asher had a friend with a missing eye, who made it a point not to wear a patch. Sort of a hostile gesture, Asher thought at the time.

"Well actually I don't even know the question, to tell you the truth," Asher says.

"Sounds like woman trouble to me," Amos says.

"Ex-wife," Asher says. "We've got this dog. *I've* got this dog." He explains. Several people at the long aluminum table stop what they're doing and listen.

"You thought about just taking the bitch to the pound?"

"Can't do that," Asher says.

"Why not?"

"Don't know," Asher says. "Just doesn't seem right."

––––––––

Barbara takes Asher up to the university film series to see *The African Queen*. In the middle of all these students, Asher feels out of place, caught in the wrong time frame. The film is terrific but he can't seem to get in the mood. Bogart and Hepburn are prisoners on the German gun-boat; the captain pronounces them man and wife, then waves at his soldiers and says "Carry on with the execution." Asher starts to laugh. Students turn around and glare at him. He feels like an idiot but he can't stop.

Afterwards they go to the Country Kitchen and Asher explains the joke while he eats ice-cream and apple pie.

"It's not funny," Barbara says.

Asher pushes his plate away and lights a cigarette. "I suppose not," he says.

The waitress takes away the plates. She's maybe eighteen, with Farah Fawcett hair and a nice smile. She could be a cheerleader. "How're you all doing?" she says.

"Pretty good," Asher says. "But it's early yet."

On the wall opposite their table there's a sort of Norman Rockwell still-life: a kitchen table with a checkered tablecloth and a bowl of red apples. The whole thing looks clumsy and good-hearted.

"How about it?" Barbara says. "We could get into your car right now. By tomorrow morning we could be in El Paso."

"Why El Paso?"

"Reno, then," Barbara says. "Idaho Falls. Cheyenne."

Instead Asher tells her about his friend Amos at the sheet-metal shop, with the little sock over what's left of his index finger, and about his friend in college who didn't wear an eye-patch.

"What's the point?" Barbara says.

"Why does there have to be a point?" Asher says.

———

He's knocking at Cindy's door. He's got Stella on a leash. The animal is excited to be in a new place and stands up with her front paws on the door. When Cindy opens it the dog falls inside.

"What is this?" Cindy says. Asher can see she's not pleased. "What are you doing here? You can't come in."

But Asher has let go of the leash and Stella is already in the living-room, her chest on the ground, her rear end up in the air, waving her tail like a pom-pom. Asher recognizes the man sitting on the couch with a drink in his hand.

"I just brought the dog," Asher says. "It's Cindy's, really."

"All right," Cindy says. "You can have one drink, then out. And you take the dog with you. This is embarrassing."

Asher sits on the end of the couch. "I'm Asher," he says. "I used to be married to Cindy here, but it didn't work out. She doesn't love me any more."

The man looks ill at ease, but he shakes hands with Asher. "LaVern Hansen," he says.

"I like your license plate," Asher says. "EGO. That's funny."

Cindy comes back from the kitchen with a glass of scotch for Asher. "I never did love him, not really," she says to LaVern. "It was a high-school thing and it sort of got out of hand."

"So you're in business," Asher says. Stella hasn't come out of the kitchen yet. He can hear her rustling around in there; he hopes she won't pee in a corner. He doesn't think she will. His theory is that the dog suspects he drove Cindy out of the house, and the peeing is a form of accusation, or maybe revenge.

"I'm a stockbroker," LaVern says.

"I bet you make a lot of money," Asher says.

"I was a cheerleader and Asher played on the football team," Cindy says.

"It's not so much the money," LaVern says. He leans forward and spills part of his drink on Asher's leg. "I'm sorry," he says.

"Forget it," Asher says. "It's an old pair of pants."

"I'm glad to see you two are getting along," Cindy says.

"It's the *science* of buying and selling," LaVern says.

"You've had your drink and you've embarrassed me," Cindy says to Asher. "Now it's time for you to leave."

"I'm sorry," LaVern says to Asher. "She's a little out of sorts tonight."

Cindy comes back from the kitchen dragging Stella at the end of the leash. The dog doesn't want to go; she's digging her feet into the carpet and whining. "Take her with you," Cindy says.

"She doesn't like me."

LaVern is kneeling on the carpet, scratching Stella behind the ears. "Good dog," he says in a high voice like the one you use to talk to babies. "Good puppy." He scratches her chest; Stella licks his hand. "I like dogs," he says.

"Out," Cindy says to Asher. "Now."

"Couldn't we keep her?" LaVern says.

"You're leaving too," Cindy says. "Out. I've had all I care to stand for one evening." She pushes both men and the dog out on the landing. They can hear her slide the bolt. "Go away."

Asher puts his ear to the door. "She's crying," he says.

"She's a wonderful woman," LaVern says. "Just a little high-strung, is all."

"I could have told you that much," Asher says.

Half-way down the stairs, dragging the dog, he looks back and sees LaVern still standing there. The stockbroker looks sad and surprised.

"She's a modern woman," Asher says. "A strong-minded person. Give her a little time to think it over."

He puts Stella in the car, closes the door, comes back to the bottom of the stairs. LaVern is sitting on the top step, holding his head in his hands. "Let's go get a beer," Asher says. "Just the three of us. I know a bar where they'll let Stella come inside."

The dog insists on being in the front seat with them. She sits mostly on LaVern's lap. Her eyes are closed but Asher knows she's awake, not feeling any better than they are about the way the evening went.

"Look at it this way," Asher says.

PRAYER FOR THE DEAD

FROM WHERE HE SITS on the roof of his sister's building Allen can see
the cars burning. They're being torched for insurance, Penny says, or maybe
just for revenge or for excitement. They make big smoky cheerful flares; it's a
celebration of chaos and disorder. On the elevated highway by the river three
guys on Japanese ninja bikes are terrorizing the commuters, doing wheelies at
eighty or ninety miles an hour between the cars. They do this every afternoon
about this time; sooner or later they'll miss a shift or hit a pothole and crash
and burn, but Allen figures they don't give a damn. Very third-world, this kind
of careless attitude about death, his sister says.

South Harlem, she says. Tanzania on the Hudson.

There's street life going on down there. Music, dope, outdoor religion.
Penny's put some folding chairs out on the roof, made a little garden in yellow
clay pots, set out tables and chairs. Tar Beach, she says.

When she and Bob moved up here they put in a bathroom, did a little sheet
rock, laid down some carpets. They bought themselves a big-screen Sony and
a CD player. Eight stories up the service elevator from what is clearly the
future of the world, they've got a private life. They manage the place, which
is a warehouse now. They do some repairs, keep track of the merchandise.
In the middle of the night when the door alarms go off on the ground floor,
Bob goes down in the elevator carrying a softball bat and checks out the dark

places. So far it's just been rats or the wind, he hasn't been knifed by a bunch of crazed dope-fiends, but what are the odds?

"Not so good," Penny says. She and Allen are lying on the roof on a silver space-blanket, sharing a joint, listening to the music and the languages coming up from below, a confused noise not too different from surf, blowing sand, wind in the trees. Natural, he thinks, until he hears the Kawasakis winding up in the distance for another death-run up the East River Drive.

Allen's friend, Melissa, killed herself last month. Speaking of death. Drove her Toyota up to the Catskills, rented a room, wrapped herself in a floppy plastic bag from the cleaners and, Allen plays the scene over and over in his head until he can't stand it, stared at the ceiling while the air ran out.

Allen tells Penny how he called up Melissa and got her answering machine. The voice, cheerful and commonplace, as if this day was no different from other days, said "I'm not home now."

"She was already dead," Allen says. "While I was listening to her tell me hello she was dead."

"I don't understand how anybody could do that to herself," Penny says.

There's a smudged crescent moon hanging over the river, a couple of stars showing through the smoke. Winking lights, meaning a jet plane on final approach to La Guardia.

"She couldn't forgive," Allen tells Penny.

"I can't forgive either," Penny says. "But if I'm going to kill myself I'll pick out something easier."

"She left this poem taped on the wall by her bed," Allen says. "By Anne Sexton."

"Pills," Penny says. "I'd take a lot of good pills and just drift off to sleep, like everyday. No big emotions."

Her voice is dreamy and soft, as if she's really saying that this would be no big thing for her. Listening to her, Allen feels a little scared.

Later his other sister, Emily, comes up to the roof to join them. She lives in Brooklyn Heights with her boyfriend. They're both musicians, trombonists. It's not a living, but they work on the side at regular jobs and they manage somehow. They have BMW motorcycles and drive around town dressed in black leathers, zipping in and out of the dense traffic like maniacs.

"You both look like gloom," she says. "What's the problem here?"

"If you were going to kill yourself," Penny says, "how would you do it?"

"On the bike," Emily says without hesitation. "I'd take it up the Thruway, you know, about a hundred and twenty miles an hour, and bam! into a bridge abutment. All over in a second."

"Or a tree," Penny says, as if she likes this idea even better than the pills.

"Wouldn't do to be just crippled," Emily says.

She stretches out on the silver blanket with Allen and Penny. They put their arms around each other and just lie there staring at the dirty moon, listening to the tropical music from about a hundred radios down below.

When their mother died of cancer Allen was the one who broke the news to Penny and Emily. He went to pick them up at summer camp; they stopped at a Ho-Jo's on the Thruway and sat in the little outdoor picnic area with their milkshakes. Tiny kids ran around doing dumb things.

It's a big deal, this death business. Nobody wants to hear about it. We all hate to be reminded.

People near them ate hot dogs and threw the wrappers on the grass. Dogs licked each other. A little wind blew car exhaust over from the parking lot.

"Is mother really going to die?" Penny said.

"No," Emily said.

"Yes," Allen said. As soon as the word was out he was sorry he'd said it. Like a knife that word had stabbed his mother in the heart. Saying yes made him a killer.

They talk about whether Bob should buy a pistol to go with the aluminum Spalding for those night patrols into the heart of darkness. Emily thinks yes. Penny says what if he killed somebody. He's a gentle person, he'd be sorry for the rest of his life.

"Even if those people would just as soon die as anything," she says. "But that isn't the point."

"What is the point?" Emily wants to know.

"Why did your friend the lawyer kill herself?" Penny says.

"Her name was Melissa," Allen says.

"Don't tell me about she couldn't forgive," Penny says. "I don't understand what that means anyway."

They can hear Bob hammering inside. He's putting up more sheet rock, dividing one big room into two little ones. He could come out and talk to them, but he's happiest when he's building something.

"You remember the summer Mom died?" Emily says.

"Nineteen sixty-eight," Allen says. "Chicago. Abbie Hoffman was on the television all the time."

"You got your hair cut," Emily says. "Mom said you looked like Marcus Aurelius."

"Nero," Penny says. "She said Nero."

"Sometimes I have a dream that she's still alive," Emily says. "In the dream it was all a mistake and she didn't really have cancer."

"All dreams are lies," Allen says.

"Hush," Emily says. She holds Allen's wrist tight. He can feel his own blood fumbling under her fingers in little jumps and starts.

———

Allen sits at the Formica kitchen table in his apartment in Queens, re-inventing himself for the morning with coffee and cigarettes and fifties rock'n roll from a local station. When the phone rings he reaches for it without looking and in his best bass, *Blue Moon* voice, says "Speak to me."

"Is that you?" Emily says. "What the hell are you doing now?"

"Rod Steiger," he says.

"Yeah?"

"*Heat of the Night*," he says. "Not a *great* film. But well done in its own way."

"Yeah," she says. "Well."

"Can't compare with some movies I've seen," Allen says. "But I do love the way he answered the phone."

Emily doesn't say anything. Allen can hear police sirens racing along Queens Boulevard. The radio in the bedroom is talking its way through the weather. The announcer is a young woman with a high nasal voice; she pronounces each word with terrible clarity and perfect timing. Every sentence falls from the radio like a little string of beads. All performance, but hell, what isn't?

"I'm all by myself," Emily says. "Don's playing a wedding in Connecticut. You want to drive over here and cheer me up?"

"Is today Saturday?" Allen says.

"Losing track of the date is the first thing that happens to crazy people," she says.

"I'm not crazy," Allen says. "A little confused, maybe." He thinks about it for a minute. "Definitely not crazy," he says.

"So are you coming over?"

"I've got a heavy day ahead of me," he says. "Things to buy. People to see."

"I'm lonely," Emily says. "I'm full of inchoate yearnings. I need a little human company."

"Lunch," Allen says. "That's the best I can do."

"Where?"

"Cornelia Street Cafe?" Allen says. "One o'clock?"

"That's the absolute best you can do, did I hear you right?"

"Don't do guilt," Allen says.

"I *never* do guilt," she says. "Lunch isn't nearly enough, but I know how to settle for what I can get."

Allen drives down Austin Street looking for Pier 1 Imports. He knows exactly what he wants: a wicker chair, one of those that looks like a throne for a minor Southeast Asian king. With arms for his arms, and a high back that will flare out above his head. A chair Sydney Greenstreet might have sat in.

"It's got to be just exactly perfect," he tells the woman in the store. She looks at him with sadness.

"Everybody always says that, but they hardly ever mean it," she says.

She takes him to the back of the store, where chairs are piled up to the ceiling.

————

Allen and Emily walk down Cornelia Street. "I'm not ready to go home yet," she says. "Let's do some shopping."

"For what?"

"Junk jewelry," she says. "I'm in the mood for junk jewelry. Maybe a pair of earrings made out of I-Ching coins. Something like that."

"I could use a copper bracelet," Allen says.

"Here," Emily says. "Hold my hand. Pretend we just met and we're about to become lovers. You're going to buy me the first present and you're wondering what it ought to be. Important to strike just the right note, you know what I'm saying?"

"Art Deco necklace," Allen says.

"Umm," she says. "No, I don't think so. Too pushy. Too much too quick. No, it ought to be something cheap but at the same time sentimental."

"Book of Wallace Stevens poems?"

She shakes her head. "I can see you need some lessons in civilized behavior." She lets go of his hand, spins herself around a parking meter, does a little two-step before she grabs his hand again. "Were you in love with Melissa?" she says.

"No," Allen says. "Yes. Maybe."

"I sense a little confusion here."

"She was the smartest person I ever met," Allen says.

He looks up between the buildings. The air this afternoon is dry and warm, almost feverish, suffused with a peculiar yellow New York gloom. Sheets of newspaper are blowing high up near the rooftops, riding the thermals like big two-dimensional gray birds.

"She was never a happy person," Allen says.

Penny calls up in the evening. Allen's stretched out on the couch reading *Popular Mechanics* and watching a rerun of *Taxi*. It's the episode where Judd Hirsch has a date with the fat girl.

"So we got ourselves a gun," Penny says. "One of the guys that stores stuff in the building let us borrow his goose-gun."

"What's a goose-gun?" Allen says. On the TV Judd Hirsch is trying to be nice but the fat girl hates him.

"It's a gun you hunt geese with," Penny says. "Forty-inch barrels. Looks like an anti-aircraft cannon. Have to turn it length-wise just to get in the elevator."

"In your opinion is Judd Hirsch the most civilized human being in the world?" Allen says.

"Are we watching the same show?" Penny says. "That's weird, you know."

"If I was fat would you still like me?" Allen says.

"If you were also gentle I would," Penny says. "Yes."

"Gentle?"

"You could have been my one and only," Penny says.

Allen is not exactly sure how seriously to take this. There was a time when he was certain he was in love with his sisters—first Emily, then later Penny, but it's been years and years.

"Let's celebrate," Allen says. He's sitting in his new Burmese king chair from Pier 1 Imports. It creaks when he moves, and he's not sure how long it'll hold him up, but for now at least he's willing to take it on faith. The light comes from a couple of K-Mart candles set in ashtrays. There's a bottle of Napa Valley red on the table, and some walnut cookies in a paper plate.

"What are we celebrating?" Penny says.

"The dark rich pageant of life," Emily says.

"You stole that line from a movie," Penny says.

"Let's have a good time," Allen says to his sisters. "Let's pretend we're all going to live forever."

A CHRISTMAS STORY

YOU'RE SITTING ON YOUR front porch in your ski parka and hiking boots and wool socks, watching the snow slant down through the streetlights. Behind you in the living room, your twelve-year old son is hunched over the coffee table drawing on a big sketch-pad you gave him last Christmas. The kid is talented, a wicked cartoonist. There are pictures of you on the walls everywhere, bearded, hair askew, a cigarette hanging out of your mouth. You haven't actually had a smoke in six months, but when you point this out to your son, he reminds you that if cartoons have a relationship with reality, it's a complicated one.

You're thinking of calling up your second ex-wife and asking her if she's any happier now than she was when she was with you, but you're afraid you might know the answer. She's a lawyer in Las Vegas, married to the man who came in second in the World Series of Poker last year. The night she walked out she told you you'd never amount to anything because you had a bourgeois mentality.

Sitting there on the old couch you put on the front porch because you couldn't bear to take it to the dump, watching Norman Rockwell snow, flakes as big as popcorn, come down, you think *maybe she was right.* You think *is bourgeois mentality a bad thing?*

The next morning you're in True-Value looking for an extension cord and some light bulbs. You've been thinking lately about replacing all the bulbs in

your house with big clear globes the size of grapefruit. Somebody told you they
don't get as hot as a regular bulbs and therefore last practically forever. On the
other hand your girlfriend wants you to buy the little screw-in fluorescent lights
that use less electricity. You're anxious to do your part to save the world, at least
slow up the greenhouse effect that's going to bake us like microwave pizza in
another twenty years, but under fluorescent light your skin turns green and you
look like the 2,000 year old man. You make a mental note to send 20 dollars to
the people saving the rain forests of the Amazon instead.

The man ahead of you in line for the cash register looks familiar and you
realize it's Jake Garn. You want to tap him on the shoulder and say "Jake, this
abortion thing's getting out of hand back there in Washington." You want to say
"Jake do you really deep down in your heart believe this stuff about the Nephites
and the Lamanites? Is Ezra Taft Benson really the Prophet? Have you talked to
God today, Jake?"

But the senator looks sort of tired and ordinary, holding his can of white
Everlasting Latex paint in one hand and fumbling his Visa card in the other, so
you leave him alone.

In the Smith's next door you buy pickles and cream cheese and paper
towels—the pure white ones that won't put undegradable dyes into the
ecosystem. You tell yourself to remember to ask for paper bags instead of plastic
at the checkout counter. You walk down the Mexican food aisle and you think
about your girlfriend and her recipe for Tofu chili. You try to imagine what
kind of world it would be if she had her way. Nicer, sure, but maybe not as
interesting. Like cartoon heaven, where everybody suffers all the time from
undifferentiated bliss.

It's Christmas Eve. Across the street your neighbor is using a snow shovel to
throw some manure on his porch roof. He does it every year; it's an old story
and you have other things to worry about. As weird and eccentric behaviors
go in this town, it's not big-time. You personally know three men who
routinely hold conversations with famous dead people. When you read that
the last certified sighting of the Wandering Jew was in Salt Lake City in 1928,
you weren't surprised. It's a National Enquirer kind of town. When your
neighbor's finished he walks back to his garage to put away the shovel and the

half-empty bag of manure from Western Gardens. In a minute he'll come out again dragging the Flexible Flyer and he'll take the kids and the wife up the block to the park for a little sledding under the lights.

You decide now might be a good time to call your ex-wife, but when you do Bernie the poker player is the one who answers. He tells you she's up in Oregon to spend Christmas with her folks. You ask him how he's doing and he spends ten minutes telling you about a hand of no limit Texas hold-em at the Stardust last night. Something about a tourist who had no business in the game beating him out of four thousand dollars with a pair of nines.

"Tell Stella I said Merry Christmas," you tell him.

"Sometimes you eat the bear, sometimes the bear eats you," he says. It takes you half a minute to realize he's still talking about the poker game.

"Man had no business staying in that long with a pair of nines," you say, trying to make him feel better.

"Stella's a good person," he says. "But she does have a temper. I guess you'd remember that."

"So are you two happy?" you ask him.

"Happy?" he says. You can tell he's thinking it over. There's some low cross-talk on the line. You can hear a woman saying something about her brother. Somebody else is laughing.

"Well I don't know about *happy*," the poker player says. "But it's not boring, you know what I mean."

He hangs up, or maybe you did. You make yourself a buttered rum in the microwave, and some hot chocolate for the kid. He's working on another picture: a guy that looks like you is talking to a turtle with a TV antenna coming out of its shell. "Must be dull being a turtle," the guy is saying. "Not if you've got cable," the turtle says. It doesn't make sense, actually, but it's funny as hell in a New Yorker kind of way, and you figure the kid's probably going to be famous when he grows up.

You'd like to still be around to see that, fame being, you suspect, one of the better things in this life. Not free of encumbrances and annoyance, naturally, but still probably pretty fine. You watch the kid take little sips of his hot chocolate; he cocks his head to look at the cartoon he's making, adds a line. You wonder how he'll handle it, being famous. If he'll be graceful.

Later you'll go upstairs and do a little gift-wrapping. The kid'll be asleep. You'll come back down and put the packages under the tree, stare at it for a while. You'll unplug the lights so the house won't catch fire while you're dreaming in your bed.

But first you'll put on the boots and the parka and go for a walk in the snow, if it's still falling. Maybe you'll meet your neighbor and his family coming down the hill a mile a minute on their Flexible Flyer. He'll be sitting in front, elegant and cheerful. Behind him his wife, her eyes closed, a dreamy expression on her pretty face, and behind her the two children clinging to her and to each other, ready as can be to hang on through bumps and disruptions they can right now barely imagine. They'll fly past without seeing you and disappear into the lovely empty brightness of the Avenues at night.

BIGGER THAN LIFE

"WANT TO SEE THE BABY?" RITA SAYS.

We're having lunch together in the Village Inn. When our marriage was breaking up we used to come here two and three times a day. All the waitresses got to know us. We hogged one of the good booths by the window and we argued about which of us was a better person. Now that we're not man and wife any more, it's not an issue.

"Take a look at this," she says.

She digs into her purse and brings out a Polaroid snapshot in black and white. I turn it this way and that; it looks like nothing, a blurry satellite photo of Saudi Arabia maybe.

"What is it?"

"Ultrasound," she says.

That thing there in the middle of the photo about the size and shape of a kidney bean, she explains, is our baby. "See that?" she says. "That's his heart."

The waitress brings Rita's tuna fish salad and my bacon burger. Her name is Cathy and she's married to a man I play poker with sometimes, a fat fiction writer who gets drunk at parties; last September at Charlie Pogue's house he got down on all fours, ran around the room barking like a dog, bit a girl on the thigh.

"How's Bill doing?" Rita says.

"He's getting his novel published," Cathy says. "We're going to be rich."

"Why does she put up with a man like that?" Rita says after she's gone.

"Love," I explain. "And if he gets famous she'll be in all the biographies."

Rita picks up a forkful of tuna, studies the color, lays it down again without taking a taste. "I'm not really hungry," she says. "I just wanted to talk to you and make sure we understand each other before I go on with this baby thing."

"I'm not changing my mind, if that's what you mean."

"I can't believe you really want to do this," she says.

I hunt around on my plate for the pickle. I eat the little black olive on the plastic toothpick. I don't want to get into an argument now.

"You were always telling me you wanted your freedom," she says. "How are you going to chase women and play cards when you've got a baby?"

The bacon burger tastes like warm cardboard but I keep chewing. I'm too thin. If I don't watch myself all the time I don't eat and then the bones start to show and pretty soon I look like one of those starving horses on the evening news, that somebody left in a field and forgot. For all I know I could die.

I watch Rita over the rim of my cup while I drink the coffee. She's still beautiful. If we didn't get along, it wasn't entirely her fault. When it comes to living with somebody I'm a dope. If I ever do the right thing, it's an accident.

"Let me get it straight," she says. "I have the baby and then you take over. I don't have to live with you or anything?"

"You don't even have to visit," I tell her.

———

This Friday night the poker game is at Charlie Pogue's house, in the same kitchen where Bill ran around on all fours and bit women. I'm holding two hidden aces and waiting for somebody else to make the first move. In the next room there's a pornographic video playing on Charlie's Mitsubishi. Sexual organs forty inches high in vivid color, disporting themselves in predictable combinations. A girl named Barbara Ann is sitting on Charlie's couch eating chocolates out of a silver box and watching the action. Nobody seems to know exactly who she is. I'd be interested, but I'm losing money just now, and trying to pay attention to the cards. Bill's already lost his money and he's sitting on the couch with Barbara Ann, looking at body parts. I hear they're going to make a movie out of his book. Maybe he'll bite people at Hollywood parties. Probably over there they wouldn't even think that was peculiar.

"You've got aces," Charlie says. "But I'm betting anyway." He shoves forty dollars worth of chips into the pot.

"Defeated are the poor in spirit," Jacob Shimmer says.

"Does that mean you're folding, or what?" Charlie says.

On the other side of the table George and Michelle are leaning sideways so they can see the happenings on the big screen. They're husband and wife, both lawyers. She does family relations; George is mostly real-estate. She's handling my baby thing with Rita. I'm supposed to meet both of them in her office tomorrow to sign the papers.

I throw in my cards, Charlie takes the money and shuffles the deck. "Anybody hungry yet?" he says. Charlie always lays out a big spread for the game—cold cuts, cookies, chips and dip, a bowl with little candies, a plate of raw vegetables.

"I'm hungry," Harvey says. "But I can't eat. The doctor says lose weight or die." Harvey is Jacob Shimmer's partner. They run a big junkyard on the West side of town, full of yesterday's cars piled up on top of each other like loaves of bread.

"Defeated are the weak of mind," Jacob says. He talks like a poet, but he's an aggressive poker player, always ready to bluff, ready to raise. Tonight he's got most of my money piled up in front of him.

"Go ahead," Harvey says. "Insult me. I can take it." He reaches for a piece of celery. "I've got a stronger mind than some people I'm looking at."

Barbara Ann wanders in from the living room holding her box of chocolates. She's wearing a white dress and a golden circlet over her hair, like an angel in a cheap painting. She looks maybe twenty years old, a little tough around the edges, but definitely attractive.

"Movie's over," she says. "Can we play it again?"

"Go ahead," Charlie tells her. "Have a good time."

"Somebody flashed me in the Smith's parking lot the other night," she says.

"Actually showed you his weenie?" Charlie says.

"If that's what you want to call it."

"Did you tell your father?" Charlie says. "He's a cop, isn't he?"

"Uh-uh," she says. "He's in the Air Force. My mother's the cop."

"So did you tell her?"

"He was an old guy," Barbara Ann says. "I think he was just feeling lonesome."

When the game breaks up I offer her a ride home. We end up at my place. She pulls the white dress off over her head and we make love lackadaisically on my living room couch. Neither of us is that interested, but it seems like too much trouble to sit and make conversation.

Afterwards she rolls to the side, props her head on one elbow and looks me over.

"I could make your wildest dreams come true," she says.

"Aren't you supposed to tell me that before?"

"I guess I forgot," she says. "You got a bathroom?"

"Down the hall and go left."

She's gone a long time. I reach for the remote and turn on the TV. "Do you know why people get nervous without any reason?" The letters are white against a blue background the color of the sky. There's a dissolve to the Dianetics book and the erupting volcano. I'm wondering why we never actually get to see L. Ron Hubbard's face.

"Your bathroom is full of boxes of diapers," Barbara Ann says.

"There was a sale."

"And baby food," she says. "You've got one wall stacked with cases of baby food."

I take her home. I've got this '56 Chevy coupe, two-tone green and white, with glasspack mufflers and tucked and rolled naugahyde upholstery. We're in a little time-warp here, driving this machine down the freeway, listening to AM radio. Barbara Ann doesn't have much to say but she slides over beside me on the bench seat and lays her head on my shoulder.

I'm remembering the hours I put in, stripping this car down to the bare chassis, cleaning oily parts in solvent, barking my knuckles on bolts that wouldn't give. I borrowed books; I learned everything. I rebuilt the engine by hand—new pistons, rings, valves. I begged for original parts from the warehouse in Detroit. Called a vice-president of General Motors on the phone person-to-person to get the right body moldings.

When I get back I flip through the channels until I find a movie I can relate to. Curt Jurgens in a submarine. Depth charges are exploding all around. "It is our job to die," Curt Jurgens says. "But I think we won't have to."

I reach for the stack of postcards I keep on the end table. I address one to the PO Box for Dianetics. "Dear L. Ron Hubbard," I write on the back. "Why is there something instead of nothing?"

————

In the baby department at Weinstock's I'm looking for the perfect playpen.

"This one folds up if you want to take the baby anywhere," the salesgirl says. "You could do it with one hand."

"It's got to be safe," I say. "I've read terrible stories in the newspaper about babies strangling themselves, things like that."

"Can't happen here," she says. She pokes her fingers through the mesh sides to show me there's no cause for fear.

"And a car seat," I tell her. "I'll need a car seat."

"Molded high-impact plastic," she says. "Three-point safety harness. Absorbent washable padding."

It looks like it would belong on the space shuttle but I buy it anyway. And the playpen.

———

I'm looking at the fish tank on the wall behind my lawyer. It's got a little miniature castle, a diver with bubbles coming out of his helmet, plastic vegetation, rocks of many colors. There's no sign of a fish.

"I thought Rita was supposed to be here."

"I wanted one more shot at talking you out of this silliness before she came," Michelle says.

I'm still looking for the fish.

"It's not even legal, probably," she says.

"What happened to the fish?" I ask her.

She makes a face. "Fungus," she says. "It was horrible to watch. That's why I put the tank back there. So I wouldn't have to."

"You could get another one."

"With no fish there's less to go wrong," she says.

I'm still trying to talk her into another fish when Rita arrives. Right away I can tell there's going to be trouble. She's got that look on her face which I have learned means she wants something from me I won't want to give.

"How's baby?" I ask her.

She sits across the office from me, on Michelle's leather couch. She's wearing her power outfit: beige skirt, white blouse, a little red tie, tweed jacket.

"Don't you worry," she says. "I'm taking good care of it. No drinking, no smoking, no caffeine, regular exercise."

Michelle gives us each a copy of the contract to read. Rita puts hers down on the couch beside her, leans back and crosses her legs. "Is it too late to add one part?" she says.

"Let's keep it friendly," Michelle says. "We're all friends here, right?"

I wait for Rita to go on.

"The car," she says. "I want your car."

"Rita," Michelle says.

"I want him to give up something he really loves," Rita says. "I just want to see if he would do that."

"You didn't even like the car."

"That's my deal," she says. Take it or leave it."

I look at Michelle. She throws up her hands. "I wouldn't want anything to do with this, if I had any sense," she says.

———

The next time I see Rita, it's Halloween. Charlie Pogue's house is full of people I know. The kitchen table is covered with newspapers and Jacob Shimmer is carving the biggest pumpkin I've ever seen, a real monster.

"Nobody knows how to do this any more," he says.

He's making the eyes with the small blade on a Swiss Army knife, cutting delicately, peeling off slivers of orange flesh. Pots are boiling on Charlie's stove; Jacob's glasses are steamy and I don't know how he can see what he's doing.

"Michelle was telling me," he says. "Are you giving her the car?"

"Maybe."

"Maybe," he says. "Well maybe is better than yes. But if you want an opinion from an old man, I'd say you're with women like you are with cards. My advice is learn to concentrate on one or the other. You'll do better."

"I saw Cathy in the living room. Is Bill around?"

"He went back home to put on a costume," Jacob says.

I look around. Everybody else is dressed normally.

"That boy's a one-man show," Jacob says. "Better than the circus."

In the living room people are dancing. Rita's turning and shuffling in the arms of a man a head shorter than she is. He looks like a precise sort of person, dressed exactly, nothing out of place. Rita looks good. The baby's showing a little, but nothing outrageous. I do a few slow steps with Barbara Ann. Today she's wearing a purple tank top and hot pants; she looks like an off-duty cheerleader. We twirl and spin on Charlie's carpet. Rita gives me a look over her guy's shoulder, one raised eyebrow. I'm a little ashamed of myself here, but I'm having a good time, I can't deny that.

"So how long were you married to her?" Barbara Ann says.

"I don't know. Four years? Five years? I didn't keep track, exactly."

"I don't think women should dance with guys that are shorter than they are," she says. "It looks funny."

The door opens; people are turning around to stare. It's Cathy's husband, dressed up as Barbara Ann—purple lipstick, the white dress, the golden circlet on his head.

"I helped him with the costume last night," Barbara Ann says. "What do you think?"

I've decided Rita can have the car. I'll buy a Toyota or a cheap Ford; it'll be a relief not to have to worry about parking lots and people who fling their car doors open without looking. If it rusts it won't break my heart.

But first I drive to Jacob Shimmer's junkyard. I know just what I want: a pair of tail lights like you used to see sometimes on cars twenty-thirty years ago, with a blue dot in the middle so when you step on the brake they shine a wonderful eerie purple. I know exactly where they are.

"You could kill yourself," Jacob says. "If you wait until next week I can get the kid with the forklift to take the car down for you."

"Got to have them today," I tell him.

He takes me in the office, sits me down under a machine-tool calendar where a girl who looks a lot like Barbara Ann is making tender eyes at an air-compressor.

He says Harvey's in the hospital. "Triple bypass," he says. "They tell me he'll be OK, but who knows?"

"Jesus," I say.

"We've been partners thirty years," Jacob says. "It's like a marriage."

We talk about marriage for a while; we drink Cokes out of green bottles. We talk about death.

We go outside and Jacob helps me carry a big aluminum ladder out of the shed. We prop it up against a stack of cars about twenty feet high. On top is a half-crushed '56 Chevy with my tail lights.

I have to open the trunk and squeeze half of me inside with a big Phillips screwdriver. If I look down I can see Jacob standing in the mud; he's shouting instructions.

"Unhook the wires first," he says.

"There's a little screw down near the bottom that you can hardly see," he says.

"You could kill yourself," he says.

The pile of cars sways every time I shift my weight. I think about what'll happen if it falls. I think about the baby. When I get down I'll put the new tail lights on my car and drive it to Rita's place. I'll give her the papers. Later I'll get the baby. I'm going to love that kid. I'll strap his new car seat on the passenger side of the Toyota I'm going to buy, and he and I will go for long drives in the mountains. After a few years, when he's old enough to listen, I'll explain to him how all this happened. By then I might have some idea.

LOST IN SPACE

"I DON'T KNOW IF I SHOULD be here," the girl says.

They're in the Village Inn; Coleman is sitting on the far side of the little table. He's having coffee and blueberry pie; she's drinking peppermint tea. Her lipstick leaves a strawberry-colored mark on the edge of the cup, like half a kiss.

"You probably don't even care," she says. "I mean why should you, really?" She's about nineteen years old, pretty in an unformed way, one chipped front tooth. The baby's not making any noise, just lying there quietly, wrapped in a blue blanket, staring at the ceiling. It's too young to resemble anybody in particular.

"For all you know I might be a crazy person," she says.

It's January, a gloomy mid-afternoon in Salt Lake City. The town is drowning in fog. People passing outside manifest themselves first as disturbances in the air, patches of dark that come clear for a second—faces, clothes, gestures—then fade out again. Two people walking a big black dog with curly hair. A little kid in a red coat, clutching a dictionary. A bearded middle-aged man holding hands with a young woman. Love, Coleman thinks. Everybody wants love.

"Why don't we forget the whole thing," the girl sitting across from him says.

Coleman leans over to take another look at the baby. It still doesn't remind him of anybody he knows. "I negotiated two divorces in this place," he says. "Proposed to my third wife in that booth over there.

She shrugs. What's that to her? History is an exotic notion, like painting yourself blue or sticking a bone through your nose. People do it, but she doesn't even want to know why.

"You sure you wouldn't like something to eat?" Coleman says.

"No thank you," she says politely.

Coleman takes another look at the baby. What's he supposed to be feeling here? He has no idea. What's he supposed to say to this girl? He studies her face until, like repeating the same word over and over, the idea of *face* becomes strange, a collection of conventionalized features that mean *beauty*, or *ugliness*, or just simply, *human*.

"I just wish your son would talk to me at least," she says.

"Did you ever stop to wonder why people have two nostrils?" Coleman says.

"What?"

"Two nostrils," Coleman says. "It doesn't make sense, if you think about it. One would do, am I right?"

The girl shrugs again. "Everybody's got two eyes," she says. "Two ears. Why not two nostrils?"

"Eyes and ears are off to the sides," Coleman says. "Down the middle we've got only one of everything. One nose, one mouth." He points at himself. "One heart."

"You're crazy," the girl says. "Are you going to talk to Leslie about the baby?"

"He's twenty-three years old," Coleman says. "I can't tell him what to do any more."

Coleman's son lives in a one-bedroom apartment in the basement of a brick house on Elizabeth Street. He keeps his place neater than Coleman. No dirty dishes in the sink, the floor vacuumed, the tables dusted. His books are on the shelf in alphabetical order by author. Leslie lived alone with his mother, Coleman's first wife, from the time he was six years old, and Coleman supposes she was the one who taught him this incredible neatness. When Coleman was married to her things were in a mess all the time. The day he packed his clothes in two suitcases and drove off in the Econoline van, he imagined the house shrugging itself into place behind him and settling down to a more orderly way of life. He never went back to find out if he was right. Now Leslie is twenty-three years old and has come to live here, a few blocks from Coleman's house. They found out that they like each other, though there's a great deal between them that necessarily remains unspoken.

"You still not smoking?" Leslie says.

Coleman shakes his head no, meaning yes. If he talks about it he'll remember how badly he wants a cigarette. That's the worst thing about quitting—not the craving, or the being irritable, or the way your fingertips go numb when you least expect it, but the certainty that there's isn't any point to life if you can't have a smoke. It's a black melancholy, Coleman thinks; Burton should have given it a chapter or two.

"What about this baby?" Coleman says.

Coleman bought himself a Sega for Christmas. He hooked it up to the nineteen-inch Sony in his living-room, and every evening if there's not a good movie on cable, he plays games. The one he likes best takes place in an empty K-Mart populated by hooded red and blue aliens who look like dwarf Carmelite nuns. Coleman's electronic self darts back and forth across the screen, shooting the aliens with a laser, dodging return fire. After he's knocked off all the aliens he finds himself alone in space facing a disembodied head. He shoots the head; it turns blue, puckers up monster lips as big as galaxies and spits balls of fire. Coleman can't kill it and sooner or later he dodges the wrong way and dies. He's been playing for weeks and hasn't made it past this level.

He thinks about being a grandfather. It seems like an enormous idea. Insurmountable. He calls his son on the phone.

"About the baby," Coleman says.

"I've told you everything I know," Leslie says.

"What if it's yours?"

"I don't think it is," Leslie says.

"Are you busy?" Coleman wants to know. "Is there somebody there with you?"

"Just Blaise," Leslie says. "We're watching a movie on the VCR."

"I'm playing *Alien Syndrome*," Coleman says.

Blaise is Leslie's girlfriend. She's pretty but she doesn't talk, at least not when Coleman's around.

"We're watching *Desk Set*," Leslie says.

"I was never in love with Katharine Hepburn," Coleman says. "She was wonderful, but in an abstract sort of way. June Allyson was the one I liked." The odd-shaped nose, the scratchy voice, had made Coleman intolerably sentimental when he was fifteen years old.

"All those movies where she was Jimmy Stewart's wife," Coleman says. "That's the kind of future I imagined for myself."

Blaise is the most self-contained girl Coleman's ever seen. Leslie's like that too. They make Coleman think of a pair of eggs. Pale and perfect. Untouchable. Arrogant in their perfection. Do they ever weep? Wake up at three in the morning the way Coleman does at least two nights out of every three, convinced they're dying of cancer, there's no God, they've wasted their life, the sun's going to blow up? Coleman's therapist says it's a matter of a certain fluid the brain generates to guard us from the razor edge of such thoughts. In the middle of the night this fluid runs low. The Greeks had a word for it, Coleman told her. The thin colorless stuff that permeates the universe, gives it meaning.

"We're not talking about the universe here," the therapist said. "We're talking about you."

"*Logos*," Coleman said.

That night Coleman dreams that he has a large bird on his shoulder. Big-beaked, brightly colored. A sort of tropical pelican. The bird talks to Coleman, goes everywhere with him. It's a bit foppish, petulant, this creature, but it's got wisdom. It's a comfort. When Coleman wakes up he's disappointed that it was only a dream.

Coleman has dinner with his third wife in the Chinese restaurant they used to go to every week when they were still married. Libby's a fine fierce woman, a professor of linguistics, a year older than Coleman. Tonight she's wearing a black dress with a lot of cleavage, as if to remind him of what he gave up.

"You look old," she says. She dips into the wonton soup for a shrimp, eats it in two crisp bites. "Are you still waking up in the middle of the night?"

"Yeah, but what if I was right?" Coleman says. "What if I *did* have cancer? What if the sun *was* going to blow up?"

Libby studies him the way a bird studies a worm, head cocked to one side, amused, greedy. "That's not the point."

"No?"

"I invented you, Coleman," she says. "I wrote you like a novel."

The meal is traditional Chinese-American syntax: after the soup, egg rolls, beef with oyster sauce, boiled rice, green tea, fortune cookies. Libby passes hers to Coleman. *The times are out of joint*, it says. Coleman breaks open his cookie, eats half while he hands his fortune to his ex-wife without looking at it.

"There's nothing written on here," she says. She shows Coleman the little strip of paper, turns it over; it's blank on both sides.

"Jesus," Coleman says.

"Maybe the sun *is* going to blow up," she says.

After dinner Coleman drives her back to her apartment. From her driveway there's a view of the valley. Libby leans over and kisses Coleman on the cheek. "So you're a grandfather," she says.

"Maybe," Coleman says. "If the girl isn't making it all up."

"What does she want? Money?"

"She hasn't asked me for any," Coleman says. The kiss bothers him—too casual or not casual enough. It signifies something, but what?

"She wants me to do grandfather stuff," he says. "Baby-sit. Take the kid to the park on Sundays. But I don't know."

"How's Blaise taking it?"

"How can I tell?" Coleman says. "The mother talks to me, I talk to Leslie, Leslie I assume talks to Blaise, and Blaise won't talk to anybody."

"I like Blaise," Libby says. "She's got character."

"She doesn't talk," Coleman says. "That's not actually the same as having character."

"She's capable of great silences," Libby says. "That's harder than you think."

"When I wouldn't talk you always said I was avoiding issues," Coleman says.

"Silence and not talking aren't the same thing at all."

"Jesus," Coleman says.

———

No matter what, Coleman can't get past the second level of *Alien Syndrome.* He gets that far smoothly enough—the little Carmelites in the K-Mart don't stand a chance—but those galactic lips shoot him down every time. After a while it's five in the morning and he gives up on the game and turns on National Public Radio to hear the peculiar news of the world. He makes coffee and toast while he listens to a Nicaraguan Contra talk about new boots from North America. Waterproof. With zippers up the side. Coleman loves the NPR sound effects. Parrots. Monkeys screeching. Pebbles rolling down hillsides. The swish and snap of tropical vegetation. He suspects it's all done in the studio. Little people in the back room crumpling cellophane, clapping coconut shells together. Zipper noises. The Contra loves his anti-Communist boots. He sounds about fifteen years old.

Coleman takes a cigarette out of the pack he bought at the 7-11 yesterday. He's smoking again; his chest hurts and he thinks cancer, or at least emphysema. If he's lucky he'll spend his last years in a wheelchair sucking oxygen out of a little bottle. He'll probably die in the Village Inn, trying to deal with an English muffin and a cup of mint tea. Maybe they'll bury him in the parking lot—the best customer they ever had.

NPR is talking to a young fiction writer from Montana who rides an elk. Or maybe he just wrote a story about somebody who rides an elk. Coleman used to write poems. Now he just plays *Alien Syndrome*. He reads some of the books Libby left behind. When he needs money he drives a cab. His needs are, on the whole, not great.

———

At the 7-11 Coleman checks out the cookie section without finding anything he really wants. The oatmeals with white icing look the best, but he was in the mood for something with more of a quick sugar-rush and today all they've got is quiet unspectacular stuff—chocolate chip, munchy peanut-butter things, different kinds of newtons, vanilla wafers. He gives up on the cookies, leafs through a couple of magazines about exotic cars, scans the book titles. A young girl in black tights with pink bands spiraling up one leg and across her chest jogs by the window. She's got an animal face: a mouth full of sharp teeth, a wolfish nose.

"Marlboros in the soft pack," Coleman says to the little dark man behind the counter. "And a Three Musketeers."

He figures if he can get a little sugar into the bloodstream quick, and then have a cigarette or two, the world won't look quite so dark.

———

Waiting in the rank of taxis at the airport, Coleman watches the big jets one after another make their impossibly slow approach to the runway. He knows, in principle, what keeps them up there, but a principle seems like a small thing to hold a couple hundred people suspended like that in the invisible and weightless air. It works now, sure, but how long are you going to depend on it? It's only, finally, an idea, a set of equations, that's keeping all these innocent people from the big crash and burn.

While he waits for a fare he reads one of Libby's books, which explains with diagrams and equations that simple systems can sometimes produce wildly unpredictable results. Coleman thinks *what else is new* but he goes on reading. There's a picture of a dripping faucet to illustrate the point. Two fat drops are hanging there, trying to decide if, when, and how to fall.

Three Japanese businessmen, one fat, two thin, are going up to Snowbird. Coleman loads the skis on the rack, throws the bags in the trunk, holds the door open for them to file into the back seat. The fat man decides to ride up front with Coleman and make conversation.

"Snowbird is a fine place," he says. "Many famous people stay there."

"I took Barbara Eden up the canyon once," Coleman says.

"*I Dream of Jeannie,*" the businessman says. "Fine show. We have it in Japan too."

Half-way up the canyon, negotiating the curves, watching out for falling rocks and early-morning drunks coming down the road, Coleman decides he needs a cigarette. The first drag, as always, gives him a little rush, makes life tolerable.

"Please not to smoke," one of the thin men says from the back seat.

Coleman pulls the cab to the side of the road and stops. "Listen to me now," he says. "This is my cab. If I want to smoke, I smoke. You have a choice here—you can sit there like good people and enjoy the ride, or you can get out and walk to Snowbird."

"We will complain," the man in the front seat says.

"Do that," Coleman tells him

Libby comes to pick up some of her books. While she's putting them in boxes, Coleman peers out the window. The man who brought her is sitting in the driveway in his red Honda, nervously revving the motor, staring back at Coleman.

"Paul's just a friend from school," Libby says.

"What's he a professor of?" Coleman says.

"Damn it, I wish you wouldn't dog-ear the pages to mark your place," she says. "It ruins the book. He's a professor of Communications. He writes screenplays."

"You sleeping together?"

Libby stacks the books neatly, one at a time, making the most of the space in each box. *Sexual Politics. Why Men Are Afraid of Women. The Peter Pan Syndrome. The Pleasure of the Text. Sex in Human Loving.* "How come you wouldn't read them when I was around?" she says.

"Living with you was like a graduate seminar that lasted six years," Coleman says.

"Celibacy's the name of the game," she says. "I'm not sleeping with anybody. Did you decide if you're a grandfather yet?"

"They're supposed to be taking this DNA test next week," Coleman says. "It's going to settle things one way or the other."

"Leslie's a beautiful boy," Libby says. "I can see why girls fall at his feet."

"Let's go in the bedroom and make love," Coleman says. "Your professor's happy out there; he can wait a little while."

She stops with a book in her hand. *The Rustle of Language.* She doesn't look at Coleman, but he can tell she's thinking it over carefully.

"The flap of a butterfly's wing in Nicaragua can cause a hurricane in Miami," Coleman says. He looks out the window. The professor's got the sunroof open; he's leaning back in the driver's seat listening to the car stereo. Coleman thinks he can make out Copeland, the Shaker hymn in Appalachian Spring.

"'Tis a gift to be simple," he says.

"I don't think so," Libby says. She's got her head cocked to one side, listening to the music.

———

Coleman truly hates the new couch his therapist bought. For one thing it's pure egg-shell white, like a celebration of chastity. For another, it's too soft, and slopes down and forward, so that Coleman spends his fifty-minute hour sliding himself back up, holding himself in. Today, half-way through the session, he gives up, takes a cushion off the couch for his head, lies on the floor.

"Why do you think you read so much?" the therapist says.

"Why do I play *Alien Syndrome* six hours a day?" Coleman says.

"Exactly."

Coleman's therapist is Jewish, intelligent, not as aggressive as Coleman would like her to be. He'd prefer to be confronted once a week, beaten up a little. There's nothing to fight here. On the other hand Coleman's previous therapist used to call him up at three in the morning, convinced he was about to do himself in with pills, pistol or razor blade. This is not perfect, but it's better.

"What about dreams?" she says. "Do you have dreams?"

Coleman tells her about the tropical pelican. "I was disappointed when I woke up," he says. "I liked that bird."

"Of course you would," she says.

Coleman considers asking her what exactly she means by that, but decides he doesn't, after all, care. He closes his eyes; the room disappears, his hands feel heavy. It's comfortable lying here not having to be attentive to anything. In his sleep he hears his therapist's voice asking questions for which there are, in his opinion, no answers.

————

The girl calls him again and insists they have to talk in person. As soon as he sits down across from her at the same old booth in the Village Inn, she gets up and hands him the baby.

"His name is DeWitt," she says. "Hold him for a minute while I go to the bathroom."

While she's gone the waitress brings Coleman his piece of blueberry pie and his Coke.

"Why do you put a little slice of lemon on the edge of the glass?" Coleman says.

"It's a code so we can tell it's a diet drink," she says. "That's a cute little boy—is it yours?"

"Maybe," Coleman says.

He clutches the kid harder than he has to, afraid it'll leap out of his arms and hurt itself. "I wish we'd met under more normal circumstances," he tells it. The kid gives him a bright toothless smile; it seems just happy to be here.

When the girl comes back she makes no move to take the child back. "You like the name?" she says.

"Sounds like a bird," Coleman says. "DeWitt, DeWitt, DeWitt."

"God, you're weird," the girl says. There's no hostility in her tone, at most a little wonder. For her it's one more fact. She sips her tea, watches Coleman.

"Last chance to get to know him," she says. "I'm moving to Encino next week
to be with my aunt. We won't bother you any more."

"I haven't been much help," Coleman says.

He likes this place—the booths upholstered in mauve and olive-green, oak
tables, glass and copper lamps with bulbs bigger than grapefruit. It's bright
and cheerful, an affirmation (he knows it's false but what the hell) that life is
fundamentally simple and fun. Also the place is often full of peculiar people. Two
tables down a thin man with a gray beard is carrying on a conversation so intense
that Coleman has to look again to make sure there actually *isn't* anybody sitting
across from him. Coleman's seen the man there before, talking passionately to
thin air. He's a fixture, like Coleman himself. Another resident eccentric.

"I've seen you driving your cab," the girl says. "Do you always wear that
cowboy hat?"

"For good luck," Coleman says. He gives DeWitt a little bounce on his knee.
The boy laughs and Coleman thinks now he really does look like Leslie in some
odd fashion, or at least like Leslie when he was that age.

"He's a sweet little kid," he says. "I wasn't really making fun of his name."

"You're OK too," the girl says. "I mean I understand; you've got a life and all
that. Things to do. You couldn't be a grandfather now."

After she's gone Coleman sits for a long time. He thinks about going over
to the man with the gray beard and giving him somebody real to talk to for a
change. If he was certain it would be an improvement he'd do it

———

Cross-legged yoga-style on the carpet in front of the Sony, Coleman clutches
the controller and jockeys his stick-figure self through the K-Mart, picking off
Carmelites, rescuing hostages. It's second-nature to him now; he doesn't have to
pay attention; his fingers do the thinking.

Last night Libby called to tell him she was giving up celibacy. "Paul's in the
bathroom washing himself," she said. "We just had the most incredible sex."

"He washes himself afterward?" Coleman said.

"He's clean," Libby said. "And he's reliable."

"I was never very good at reliable," Coleman said.

"It's my fault," Libby said. "I wrote you, but I wrote you badly. You were a
first draft."

Coleman shoots two more nuns; the screen blacks out and there he is floating helpless in the illimitable wastes of space, facing The Head. It puckers its lips as if to give him a galactic kiss; instead it spits fireballs. Coleman dodges but he knows it's no use. Coleman is downright nimble up there on the screen, more agile than he ever could be in real life, but all the hopping and skipping in the world won't save him now.

The speaker plays a simple electronic waltz in three-quarter time and Coleman pushes buttons, flings himself around the black sky, left and right, up and down, thinking about Libby and her professor, about his maybe grandson, about Leslie and Blaise, who could be twins. What do they think about? What do they know? How can they be so perfect?

FRACTAL GEOMETRY

WHEN THE PHONE RINGS, you're flipping back and forth on the cable TV between a documentary on Hitler's Russian campaign and the Braves-Dodgers game on America's station,

"I don't think we should see each other any more," Maria says.

You say *OK*.

"I'm young and alive and full of hope and aspirations," she says. "You always make groaning noises when you get up off the couch."

The Germans and the Dodgers are both losing, neither one with any particular grace. Dale Murphy hits a home run. Hitler makes a speech. Those compound German words fly out of his mouth and circle over the crowd like vultures.

"Are you listening to me?" Maria says.

You say *yes*. You say *goodbye*. You feel sad. You remember the good times.

You also feel like a new and wonderful person. You think tomorrow you'll call up an elegant woman and ask her to breakfast.

One afternoon not much later, you're in Costco looking at built-in dishwashers. The salesman is explaining about pre-heating coils, economy cycles, nozzle velocity. Facing you on the far side of the dishwashers is a display of camcorders, and if you raise your head you can see yourself in one of the monitors, bending over to peer inside a Whirlpool, a foolish expression on your face.

"You couldn't go wrong with this baby," the salesman says.

You think what a pleasure it would be to slip your dirty dishes in there and push a button or two. You wonder if the salesman realizes that he's making a little hungry humming noise in his throat as he watches you.

"Everybody needs a dishwasher," he says.

The store has a whole wall of televisions, all tuned to the same channel. You watch a hundred Phil Donahues talking sincerely to a hundred of the same slight, doubtful-looking young man about the possibilities of sex in prison. You think you'd like to have a television for every room in your house, reporting the condition of the world.

———

"Fractal geometry," the woman you're having breakfast with says. You're sitting across the table from her at the Market Street Broiler. It's a high-tech eating place, decorated to look like the inside of a refrigerator. All the surfaces are white and slick. You have to struggle to keep from slipping out of your seat and sliding under the table.

"Matter is a series of localized tendencies to exist," she says.

You wonder briefly what you're doing here talking to this person. She's elegant and you desire her, but is that enough? You think maybe yes.

"Don't you love this place?" she says. "Everything is so...oh, I don't know... *clean*."

Across the aisle from you, you recognize a local TV newscaster. He's sitting with a middle-aged woman who hasn't stopped talking since you sat down. You try not to listen, but you're fascinated by the lack of pause or punctuation. It sounds like she's spending her days in the middle of the same life-long sentence.

"The food's not bad," you say. "A little too creative, maybe, but OK."

"Creative?" she says.

"Spices. I think they've got this guy in the kitchen that's crazy about spices. He has ambitions."

She laughs politely and you suspect she thinks you're a fool. She has blond hair, cut very short. You wonder how old she is.

———

You go to the supermarket with a vague yearning for green grapes, or maybe peaches. Instead you buy a ten-pack of Three Musketeers in the new space-age Mylar foil wrappers. You stop at the pharmacy counter and sit down at the blood-pressure machine. You finally figure out the instructions and get things rolling. The cuff closes around your upper arm; after a while the little numbers tell you you're in no immediate danger, but still maybe you should cut down on the salt, and exercise now and then.

You check out the magazines and buy one with an article on fractal geometry. It has a beautiful picture on the front cover—an odd-shaped black center surrounded by an intricate reticulated web of colors. Somehow it looks *real*. Not like a *picture* of anything, you decide, more as if it was the visible articulation of some perfectly profound truth.

In the meat section you buy a whole chicken, some turkey wings, a package of ground beef. For a while last year you decided to be a vegetarian. It was a moral issue, not eating living things. But then you began to wonder where to draw the line. Eggs? Cheese? What about things that didn't seem to have all that much consciousness, like the lower kinds of fish? Are oysters part of the moral universe? Squid? Gradually you went back to eating meat and simply trying not to think about it.

You buy a book of stamps from a girl who reminds you of Maria, but who has a nicer smile. There was always something too complicated about Maria's smile, as if it allowed itself to appear only after several levels of irony had been temporarily resolved.

You pay for everything with a check and are absurdly pleased when the woman at the register recognizes you and doesn't ask to see your guarantee card.

Maria calls and asks you to dinner at her place. You think it's probably a bad idea but you say yes anyway. She makes a *salade niçoise*, with black olives, tomatoes, chick peas, tuna fish. You drink white wine with the dinner, and try to make small talk. She looks especially beautiful tonight, you think.

You make love afterwards, and then lie in bed together watching *Mutiny on the Bounty*, with Clark Gable and Charles Laughton. It's the computer-enhanced version, but you turn the color all the way down and it doesn't look too bad.

"Which part of my body do you like best?" Maria says.

You're a little confused here. You thought it was all over between you, but there you are in bed, clinging to each other like small animals, licking and nuzzling. What's going on, exactly? You don't want to ask.

"Is that a difficult question?" she says. She lifts the sheet so you can have a good look. "Take your time," she says.

There's a moment of panic when everything you think you might say sounds stupidly erotic, like the time you were shown Rorschach blots by your high-school guidance counselor. You get hold of yourself by taking a minute to watch Captain Bligh order a hapless sailor keelhauled. It's a more complicated process than you would have imagined, with blocks and tackles, ropes and intricate lashings. The sailor dies.

"Your breasts," you say. "I love your breasts."

You both watch the movie for a while. It's true that Bligh is an evil person, perhaps insane, but you're not certain that Clark Gable is entirely innocent. There are higher moral questions at stake.

"Aren't you going to ask me which part of your body I like?" Maria says.

"OK, which?"

Instead of telling you, she turns her head away. "I've missed you," she says. "But we're doing the right thing."

You wish you knew what she was talking about.

———

Your landlord invites you to a Tupperware party. He's a deeply religious man and the only thing there is to drink is red or green punch made with Kool-Aid; little slices of fruit float in the punchbowls. You thought that Tupperware parties were a gender-related activity, but when you get there you realize that at least half the guests are men. Among them you recognize the TV newscaster you saw in the restaurant. All these people know each other from church, and it occurs to you that your landlord invited you as a sort of reclamation project. He thinks you're wasting your life. First Tupperware, then conversion, seems to be the plan.

You buy three nesting bowls and a big box in which you can put away your sweaters for the summer. You like the texture of the plastic, smooth, dense, resilient. You like the promises that are part of the transaction—these things will never leak, will remain forever airtight, will never never wear out.

You pull your landlord aside. His name is Frederic; he's drinking a cup of green punch.

"Coffins," you say. "Tupperware coffins. They'd be perfect. Think about it. We could make a fortune."

He pulls you aside into an alcove, sits down beside you.

"How much do you know about the Mormon Church?" he says.

———

Your friend Barry wants to take you to Studebaker's so you can meet women. It's on the ground floor of the Chamber of Commerce building; there's a cherry-red 1949 Commander convertible displayed in the window; they play disco music.

"The women there are beautiful," he says. "And they're professional women; they've all got jobs."

You tell him you'd rather stay home and watch *Borsalino* on the arts channel. Alain Delon. Jean-Paul Belmondo. Marseilles.

"You could get laid," he says. "Doesn't that sound like more fun?"

You tell him you've made a new resolution to go to bed only with women you actually like.

"You'd like these women," Barry says. "Going to bed with professional women is incredible. At first they're so dignified and powerful, controlling, you know? But then they let go of all that and it's…"

"What?"

"Intimate?" he says. "That's not the right word. I don't know, but they're better than ordinary women. It's like they're giving you something infinitely precious," he explains.

You end up watching *Borsalino* together. You like the old cars, the Thompson machine guns with round magazines, the dance of complicated betrayals, the sentimentality of gangsters.

———

"Maybe we should get married after all," Maria says. "If you die, you die, right? I mean I could get run over by a streetcar tomorrow, then you'd be the one who's left alone."

You're sitting in the Village Inn. She's eating the Spanish Skillet, with eggs and red chili peppers and salsa. You're having the fresh strawberry pie and some not very good coffee.

"What happened to hope and aspirations?" you ask her.

"Still there," she says. She holds up a forkful of egg dripping with red salsa. "Doesn't that look damn near edible?" she says.

Your waitress walks by but you give her a look that says *not now* and she moves on without asking you how everything is today.

"If you go and feeble out on me after a few years I guess I'll just have to deal with it, won't I?"

She gives you the complicated smile. You think maybe you ought to walk out now, before it gets any worse. The light hanging over the table is getting in your eyes, but you tried unscrewing the bulb the last time you were here, and the manager came over and gave you a serious lecture on customer safety. You can see him right now, behind the cash register, a young guy in a brown polyester suit, with a red bow tie. He was born for this job, one of those people who've found their exact place in the world.

Maria's looking at you. "Hey, I think I just proposed ," she says. "So how about it? Yes or no?"

You feel somehow out of sequence here, as if you'd slept though part of the movie and woken up to find the characters doing incomprehensible and unnatural things. You think about Jean-Paul Belmondo flipping his two-headed coin with that little mysterious smile, and Alain Delon smoothing the brim of his new hat with thumb and forefinger.

You say *no*.

NATIONAL GUARD

AT THE FAR END OF A sequence of archways that looks like one of those early Renaissance paintings when artists first fell in love with perspective, Warner can see the diminished figure of his wife dancing with Carl the insurance man. Carl has on his powder-blue leisure suit; Helen is wearing camouflage fatigues.

The inside of Osterreiker's house is a Spanish fantasy in white stucco and red floor-tile, with dark oak furniture that looks like it's been beaten with chains and dipped in corrosive chemicals. On the walls are pistols, swords, pikes—the instruments of war. Later in the evening, Warner knows, Osterreiker will be demonstrating their use to four or five interested girls from the office.

"Gender reversal," Marshall says, coming up behind Warner and putting a hand on his shoulder. He's watching the dancers. "Isn't that Helen?" he says.

Marshall has the cubicle down the hall from Warner. His specialty is writing TV commercials in which unattractive people eat crunchy foods loudly and talk with their mouths full. He agrees with Warner that the ads are repulsive. He's writing a novel and shows Warner parts of it from time to time. In the novel, people eat crunchy foods and talk with their mouths full.

"I didn't know this was a costume party," he says.

"It's not a costume," Warner says. They watch Helen sway and shuffle in the arms of the insurance man. "She joined the National Guard last month,"

Warner says.

"No joke?"

"Not to me, anyway," Warner says.

Why she wanted to wear her fatigues to the party, Warner isn't sure. Theater, maybe. They've been married two years and Warner hasn't yet come to the end of her sense of the dramatic. Right now she's doing an elaborate dip with Carl; he's bent over her, almost lip to lip, his slightly horsy face full of delight.

"She looks like an Angolan guerilla," Marshall says. "Lethal, you know what I mean?"

"She's a good person," Warner says.

"I don't know how she can dance with those boots on."

"Leave it alone, OK?" Warner says.

It's a lousy party and he lives across the street; he could go home and watch Crime Story on the TV. Warner likes the old cars, and he likes the cigarettes everybody on the show smokes without worrying about anything worse than tobacco breath or a little emphysema.

"I wrote another chapter last weekend," Marshall says. "I'll bring it in for you tomorrow." He gives Warner's shoulder a quick squeeze. "I think I'm really on to something with this book," he says. "I could become rich and famous here."

"Who are these people?" Warner says.

"We'd better circulate," Marshall tells him. "Osterreiker doesn't like it if we don't circulate."

Warner walks down the sequence of archways toward the dancers. He steps over a girl in leather sitting on the floor holding hands with an older man he's seen around the office. "Excuse me," he says.

Helen is his second wife. He married her because this time he wanted beauty, intelligence, a vibrant person. He tells himself now that he got what he deserved. He stops when he gets to the edge of the dance floor. She's out there in the middle doing some sort of complicated reggae thing with Carl. People are standing in a circle around them, clapping hands.

Warner feels himself hugged from behind. It's Osterreiker. Warner wonders why everybody's being so touchy-feely tonight.

"Some kind of fashion statement, is it?" Osterreiker says.

Warner explains about the National Guard.

"She did?" Osterreiker says. "Why would she do that?"

"Told me she wanted a life of her own," Warner says. "Do you know what that means?"

"It means trouble," Osterreiker says. "If it was my wife..."

"But it isn't," Warner says.

The next time somebody hugs him, it's Helen. Warner is sitting by himself in Osterreiker's den, watching the little five-inch black and white TV. Crime Story looks even better in black and white. Torrillo is driving the empty night spaces of Nevada in a big Chrysler 300 with the top down, listening to the Platters. Warner is thinking he'd like to be there with him right now, sitting in the passenger seat, talking about the things they talk about on the show when they're not shooting people. They have the kind of serious conversations about life Warner feels he could really get into.

"You having a good time?" Helen says.

She slides over into his lap, kisses him on the ear. "Why don't you come out and dance?" she says. "You dance divinely."

"Divinely?" Warner says.

"You make everything into a question," she says. "At least come out and talk to people. It's embarrassing, you in here all by yourself."

Before Warner can think what to say to that, she's gone. The TV's doing a station break with local commercials. An enormous woman with a face like a Hereford is slurping ice-cream into her mouth. The noise reminds Warner of the sounds the animals make when they eat each other on the PBS nature shows.

When they get home Warner gets in bed first and watches his wife look at herself in the big mirror over the dresser. She twirls around, admires herself over her shoulder. "Do I look phenomenal, or what?" she says.

"Surprised a few people with that outfit," Warner says.

"Osterreiker's a jerk," she says. "I've got style, that's what I've got. I don't understand how you can go on working for that man."

She strips off the fatigues, the black underwear, and gets in bed beside Warner.

"Has Carl got style?" Warner says. "In your opinion?"

"Is that supposed to mean something?" Helen says. She's up on one elbow, looking down at Warner. "You think maybe I'm having a thing with Carl on the side?"

"It's possible."

"You really act ignorant sometimes," Helen says. "I would have danced with you if you'd come out there. Besides Carl can't have sex. Some sort of medical thing."

"He's got three kids," Warner says.

"It happened after that," Helen says.

"He told you?"

"I've got friends," she says. "I talk to people."

After she's asleep Warner lies awake, his hands behind his head, staring out the window at the streetlight. He thinks about getting out of town. Two or three times a year he takes a cheap flight to Las Vegas and plays in the five and ten dollar poker games. Most often he loses, but he likes the action, the possibility. The casinos are full of people who're not like him at all, and he likes that too.

About three in the morning Osterreiker's dog begins to bark. Warner listens for a while, then he reaches over and shakes Helen by the arm until she sits up.

"You're having an affair with Carl, aren't you?" he says.

There's an almost full moon shining in the bedroom window. Osterreiker's dog takes a deep breath and barks some more, a sequence of high-pitched yelps, as if somebody had him by the throat.

"Don't you think this jealousy thing's getting a bit out of hand?" Helen says.

"Only if it isn't true," Warner says.

Helen pulls her hair down over her face, then parts it with two fingers to look at Warner. "Give me a little room to be somebody here," she says.

Warner drifts gradually back to sleep. He dreams he's riding a big motorcycle through the desert at night, headlight turned off, only the moonlight to show him the road, a hundred and twenty miles an hour through the dark. Ahead of him somewhere is Torillo in the Chrysler 300; it's the most important thing in the world that Warner should catch up before they come into Las Vegas.

He wakes up with Helen's hands around his throat; her thumbs are up under his jaw, pressing in. Warner can breathe, but only a little.

"Being married to you is no joke, you know," she says. "Didn't I tell you he was impotent?"

"I guess I just forgot," Warner says.

———

Riding the elevator on the way up to Carl's office, Warner focuses on the little numbers over the doors. Next to him is a fat woman he could swear was the one eating ice cream in Marshall Molder's commercial.

"Beethoven's Ninth," she says.

"Excuse me?" Warner says.

"Beethoven's Ninth," she says. "That's what you were humming. The choral part. I've got it on a CD at home. I listen to it all the time."

"I didn't know I was humming," Warner says. "I'm sorry."

"It's supposed to be about Beethoven entering paradise," the woman says. "I always wondered how God would take it. I mean all that singing and all that fuss, you know? If I was God I might be offended."

Carl's secretary says he's on the phone but to go right in. Warner sits down on the near side of the desk and waits for Carl to be done with his conversation, which seems to be an argument about water damage. There's a wooden duck on Carl's desk; Warner remembers seeing a PBS show about one particular kind of duck which flies faster than any other bird. Two hundred miles an hour, or something like that. Carl's duck doesn't look like it would be the one.

"Woman left the water running in her bathtub and brought down her whole living room ceiling," Carl says. "Her own damn fault but we still have to pay."

"Tell me something," Warner says. "Am I humming, right this minute?"

Carl listens carefully; his face is friendly and concerned. "I don't hear anything."

"I was in the elevator," Warner says, "and this fat woman told me I was humming."

"I take the stairs now so I can get the exercise," Carl says. "But I remember how it was in the elevator. Flashers, missionaries with pamphlets they want you to read, people that talk to themselves."

"Or hum and don't know it," Warner says.

"Modern life makes people crazy," Carl says. "Don't tell me about it. I'm on the telephone all day with people that ought to be locked up somewhere where they couldn't bother anybody."

He arranges the papers on his desk, straightens the duck so it's staring at Warner with a yellow glass eye. It's a beautiful duck, Warner thinks. Probably hand-carved. Expensive.

"Was there anything in particular you wanted?" he says.

"Yeah," Warner says. "But it's sort of embarrassing."

Carl looks interested. He leans forward over the desk, the horsy face full of expectation. "I'm your friend," he says. "You can tell me."

Warner reaches into his pocket, pulls out a folded piece of paper; he smooths it on the desk, pushes it across to Carl. It's a one-line note.

Helen, my love for you is inexhaustible.

"Looks like your handwriting," Warner says.

Carl nods two or three times. "That's embarrassing all right." He picks up the duck, sets it down again. "I can see we've got a situation here," he says.

"Situation?" Warner says.

Carl pushes his chair back and stands behind the desk. "You're not going to get violent or anything, are you?"

"Violent?" Warner says.

He picks up the wooden duck by its beak and smashes it against the corner of Carl's desk. Wood splinters fly. The neck breaks off and Warner finds himself holding a duck's head. The top of it is painted a serious electric blue, the beak orange. Eyes made out of yellow glass.

"I'm not a violent person," he says. "You got a cigarette there?"

"You don't smoke."

"I used to," Warner says. "Before I knew you." He takes a deep drag, lets the smoke curl back out of his mouth as easily as if he'd never stopped. "Now I remember why I used to like it so much," he says.

He puts the duck head in his pocket. When he gets to the door he turns back. Carl hasn't moved. "Inexhaustible?" Warner says.

———

"Come on," Helen says. "You're not going to tell me you believe this? A guy that wears leisure suits?"

"I believe it," Warner says.

"Even if it was true," Helen says, "it wouldn't be the end of the world."

She gets out of bed and stands there naked for a minute, looking down at Warner and his cigarette. "Every one of those is seven minutes gone from your life," she says.

"Maybe," Warner says. "But you have to figure it's the *last* seven minutes and how much fun are they going to be anyway?"

"So what's next?" she says.

"I love you."

"I knew that already," she says.

She's laying out her uniform for tomorrow, which is Monday; she has to be at the National Guard Armory at six-thirty. She'll be gone all day. Fatigue blouse, pants dyed in random-shaped patches of sand and olive-green. She sits down on the edge of the bed to shine her boots, spits on the toe and rubs in the saliva with a fuzzy cloth. Osterreiker's dog is howling in harmony with a police siren in the distance. Helen is humming the choral part of Beethoven's Ninth. Warner lies back with his arms behind his head and listens. In his mind here it's Warner entering paradise, the path lined with choirs of angels and formally dressed men playing strings and woodwinds. If God's offended by all this fuss over one good person, he's not talking.

CARELESS LOVE

I'M STANDING IN THE checkout line at Smith's Food King, reading the National Enquirer headlines, PREACHER EXPLODES DURING SERMON, TENNESSEE WOMAN MARRIES FROG, when this bug comes out of nowhere and bites me on the knuckle. The pain is incredible. I think about the chances of dying right here in line, behind the fat woman with the ten thousand coupons and the skin-head with the tank-top and the jailhouse tattoos on his biceps.

"You all right?" the woman behind the register says.

I take my finger out of my mouth where I had put it for comfort, and show her where I was bitten.

"You'd think you'd be safe in the checkout line at Smith's," I tell her. My finger looks like something you'd see at the circus, on one of the clowns; already it's blowing up like a balloon; the pain is shooting clear up to the elbow.

"Yuck," she says. "That's ugly."

"That's nothing American did that," the woman with the coupons says. "Must have been some foreign bug that came with the bananas. I've heard about those."

"Tarantula," the ex-con says behind me. His cart is piled up with about a hundred six-packs of Jell-O pudding in the little transparent plastic containers. He's got all the flavors. Nothing else in there. "I know a guy got bit by one of those once," he says. "'Swelled up and turned blue and in twelve hours he was cold stone dead."

When I get home I swallow four aspirins and soak my hand in cold water.
I'm listening to T-Bone Walker singing sad songs of love and despair on the
stereo. I decide I'll call up Elizabeth and tell her about it.

"Still hurts, does it?" she says.

"Like a bastard."

"We feeling a little sorry for ourselves?"

"I suppose." T-Bone is singing about evening trains, fickle women; he's asking
questions I have found it's generally better not to ask.

"Want to talk about it?" Elizabeth says.

"I'm in favor of the unexamined life," I tell her. "Look at existence too closely
and you're apt to find out things you don't want to know."

"Is that sort of a general statement?" she says. "Or are we talking about you
and me here?"

It's become our habit to talk in riddles. I am never certain, whether I am in
her actual presence or simply on the far end of the telephone, what it is she is
trying to tell me. Lately I am not certain what it is I might mean either, at any
given moment.

I have this friend named Ross who had all his teeth pulled by a cheap dentist
when he was about eighteen years old and he fell in love with nitrous oxide.
It didn't occur to Ross until it was too late that there were other ways. This
afternoon Ross and I are driving down State Street looking for truth and beauty,
which are not, no matter what anybody tells you, anywhere near the same
thing. We pull up at a red light; an old guy in cerise pants, a green guayabera
shirt and an actual sombrero, crosses the street in front of us. He's wearing
huaraches and has a little spiky white beard, carefully trimmed. He looks quite
happy with his condition.

Ross shades his eyes to get a better look. "The only possible explanation for
this is parallel universes," he says.

We're doing the thrift stores, looking for meaningful and resonant junk. Ross
makes paintings with things like worn-out sneakers or chrome faucets glued on
the canvas. He's been doing it for about twenty years. The art world has moved
on to other notions, but Ross doesn't see any point in changing for the sake of
change. He sells a picture now and then, drives cab four nights a week, appears to

be getting through life all right. On the whole maybe more gracefully than me.

I tell him this while we're in the Disabled Veterans, pawing through a big plywood bin full of women's underwear. Ross listens to me, then he pulls a pair of peach-colored panties over his head, peers at me through one leg hole.

"Gracefulness is all there is," he says. He reaches in his mouth, pops out his dentures, clicks the plastic teeth together, does a high-pitched Richard Widmark psycho laugh. A woman with a crew-cut is coming down the aisle. She stops to stare at the spectacle.

"Well maybe it isn't *all*," Ross says. "But it's a major part."

"As an everyday normal thing, I can appreciate repulsive," the woman says to Ross. "But it could be you've just now taken it a little too far."

Ross slides his teeth back in and uses all of them to give her the big boyish plastic smile. "God is love," he says. They high-five each other.

The woman takes him by the hand and they walk off toward the used furniture section. She's about three inches taller than Ross; she has on jeans and a white T-shirt with ONCE A BITCH ALWAYS A BITCH written across it in red capital letters.

Later we all swing by and pick up Elizabeth and go to Crown Burgers for lunch. At the next table three young fat guys in short-sleeved white shirts are talking about municipal bonds, waving their pudgy hands and being passionate about percentages and discounts.

"Sidney here," Ross says with a certain discoverer's pride, "doesn't believe that she has an unconscious mind."

"Is your name really Sidney?" Elizabeth says.

"The unconscious comes from repressing things, am I right?" Sidney says.

"Isn't she something?" Ross says.

Elizabeth shakes her head. "Yeah," she says. "But *Sidney?*"

"Uh-oh," the woman says. She puts down her bacon burger and wipes her lips with her napkin. "I sense a little hostility ." She punches Ross on the shoulder. "Are we secretly in love with my man here? Is that the story?"

"Just making conversation," Elizabeth says. "Small-talk. Like, you know, being civilized."

Sidney considers this for a minute. When she frowns it's like she's got one eyebrow going across her forehead, sort of a Mariel Hemingway look, but not unattractive. "Nope," Sidney says finally. "I know conversation when I hear it. That wasn't it."

"Sidney," Elizabeth says, not addressing her but just saying it as if speaking to the air.

"You known her long?" Sidney says to me. "Never mind. Tell me about Ross and his teeth. Is this nitrous oxide business the actual truth?"

"It wasn't just the thrill of getting high," Ross explains. "I had visions. God. Aristotelian logic made visible. Dead souls. That's worth a couple of teeth, wouldn't you say?"

"Thirty-two," Sidney says. "To be precise."

"Yeah, well now we're just talking numbers here. Sitting in that dentist's chair I made distinctions like you wouldn't believe. I *understood* things."

"*Sidney*," Elizabeth says again the same way.

"You couldn't by any chance control her, could you?" Ross says to me.

Sidney finishes her burger and stands up. "Ladies room," she says. "Come on, Elizabeth, we'll talk this out in private. Without these two oafs."

The young fat guys at the next table stop talking about tax-free government issues long enough to watch the two women walk away. For a fraction of a second all three fat faces have this identical look of melancholy and hopeless generalized lust, as if they've just all realized that never in this life will they ever go to bed with two such women at the same time. One more adolescent dream gone to dust. I could almost feel sorry for them.

"Shootout in the ladies room?" Ross says.

"My guess is knives," I say. "You know, each of them holding one end of the handkerchief."

But they're coming back already, hand in hand, with tender eyes for each other and, for us, studied and severe looks.

"I think I'm in the mood for a movie," Elizabeth says.

"*Dead Poets* or *Batman*?" Ross says.

"*Great Balls of Fire*," Sidney says. "I think Jerry Lee Lewis is a great man."

But that turns out to be gone out of town already, so we end up seeing Batman for the third or maybe fourth time. Afterwards we get ice-cream cones and walk around Trolley Square. Sidney and Ross are just ahead of us; she's got one arm around Ross, her hand stuck in the back pocket of his jeans.

"She's way too good for him," Elizabeth says.

———

The two of us are lying in my bed watching the mad nun on the Catholic network. She's talking about The Last Temptation of Christ, and hinting seriously that doing violent things to theaters that show the movie wouldn't be a sin, necessarily. She tells how Jesus whipped the money-changers out of the temple. When she says *whip* her eyes glisten.

"Didn't you use to be Catholic?" Elizabeth says.

"He took a rope," the mad nun says, "made knots in it, lashed the evil out of them." She looks happy.

It's a hot night; I've got one of those nifty electric fans from the K-Mart that swivel back and forth but we're sweating anyway. The bedroom windows are open and we can hear the regular night-noises—crickets, my neighbor's dog whining, lawn-sprinklers, somebody's radio.

"If you're going to break my heart," Elizabeth says, "do it now. Don't wait until I get too attached to you."

I don't know what to say, so I switch off the mad nun and flip through the channels until I get to MTV, which is showing the documentary on Woodstock. Not as many naked people as one would imagine. Lots of folks striking different attitudes. Somebody demonstrating Kundalini yoga; three hundred thousand people doing the Breath of Fire at the same time.

"I wish I'd been there," Elizabeth says.

"Why would I break your heart?" I ask her.

Instead of saying anything she rolls over and puts her head in the pillow. In a minute she's crying.

"Hey." I touch her shoulder; her skin's hot and damp; she's trembling.

"I'm sorry," I say.

It's my fault, all this confusion, all this sadness. I try to explain.

"It's just ordinary despair," she says. "Nothing to get upset about."

———

"There's a connection between all these things," Ross says. We're sitting in the Roasting Company; the coffee of the day is a Nigerian blend which tastes like mud and dry grass. Ross is explaining about himself and Sidney, me and Elizabeth.

"It's not just a bunch of random events," he says, "but it's not your normal everyday cause and effect either."

"What is it then?"

"Something darker," he says.

The courthouse is just across the street and we're surrounded by young lawyers in ugly suits. They look like they're suffering from ordinary despair too, but in them it takes the form of greed and agitation, a sort of jumpy melancholy that drives them to do things they wouldn't do otherwise.

"What could be darker?" I ask Ross.

He ignores me. He's looking at the lawyers. "Chimpanzees," he says. "Any minute they're going to be sexually attacking each other to decide which one is going to be the boss monkey."

I can see he's getting worked up. If I don't distract him he's going to take out his teeth in a second, and get us thrown out of here. Already something edgy in his voice has caught the attention of the girl behind the pastry counter and she's giving us a hard look.

"What could be darker?" I ask him.

"Well," he says, "I know what you mean. Cause and effect is a bitch. Ask anybody. But this is truly worse. Gravity. Twists in the fabric of space and time. What am I talking about?"

"You and me and Elizabeth and Sidney?"

"Yeah," he says. "Well you didn't *have* to go to bed with her. A little self-denial and repression wouldn't have hurt."

We pay up and go for a walk. It's only about ten o'clock but the heat is fierce; I feel like all of me is evaporating into the relentless white sky above the city. On the Chamber of Commerce building somebody has hung a hand-lettered banner maybe a hundred feet long: GIVE HUGS NOT DRUGS. Ross walks with his head down, eyes focused on the sidewalk like he's looking for loose change.

"Did you?" he says. He steps in front of me so I have to stop, and pokes me in the chest with one finger. "Did you?"

I'm waiting for him to go on and hit me, but he doesn't. We go into a 7-11 and buy Slurpees to kill the taste of the Nigerian coffee. I get a fluorescent blue one that looks like Windex made into slush. It tastes artificial and wonderful.

"How's your finger?" Ross says.

I hold it up for him. It's pretty much back to normal now, except for a little brown dot about the size of a period at the end of a sentence.

APRIL, MAY, AND SO ON

SPRINGTIME IN SALT LAKE CITY, the new Zion, suburbia by the lake. New leaves on the trees, yellow flowers poking up out of last year's dead grass, the smell of rain. All the usual resurrection and renewal stuff. Carlton sits in the Roasting Company with his friends, watching the courthouse across the street, the lawyers come and go. He's holding hands with Melody. Susan and Eileen are drinking their coffee in small sips. Eileen is talking to Melody about the philosophy of computer languages. At the next table a seventeen-year old girl decked out like a fresh widow—black dress, black hat, black veil—sits across from a graduate-school Oscar Wilde in knee-high black boots and a red silk bathrobe.

"I think they're serious," Susan says.

"If you want to get into artificial intelligence in a meaningful way, there's nothing but LISP," Eileen says.

Oscar Wilde leans across the table to talk to the post-pubescent widow. "Some people think I'm a Satanist," he says, "but really I just admire the symbol system."

"I think Jung is the greatest mind who ever lived," the widow says.

"Compared to Levi-Strauss he was shit," Oscar Wilde says. He's wearing an inverted silver crucifix dangling from his right ear; when he leans forward it stays perfectly still, pointed like a pendulum at the midpoint of the earth, the center of gravity, which the Greeks called love.

"Compared to Levi-Strauss, *everybody* is shit," he says.

Susan and Eileen are rubbing knees under the table. Every few seconds Susan touches the tattoo she had done yesterday on her upper biceps. Gothic black letters that say *TATTOO*. No heart, no flowers, no dagger, no snakes. Just the one word.

"Doesn't it itch?" Carlton says.

"I could have had a butterfly," Susan says. "The man was desperate to give me a butterfly."

Eileen points to Oscar Wilde. "God, I *know* that kid," she says. "His mother and my mother are friends. He used to come over to the house with her when I was in ninth grade."

"He's cute," Melody says.

"You thought Reichler was cute," Carlton says. "But he treated you like a dog."

"Reichler had toxic parents," Melody says.

"The kid was always wanting me to go into the closet with him and play doctor," Eileen says.

"Did you?" Susan wants to know.

"Just one time."

"What about object-oriented languages?" Melody says. "They say you can do anything you want with them, if you're smart enough."

"He had this enormous erection," Susan says. "At least it looked enormous to me at the time. It had, like, veins."

"You've got a yearning for bad men," Carlton says to Melody. "Bikers. Hoods. Gas-station guys. People like Reichler."

"He wanted me to touch it," Eileen says. "I told him I'd rather be dead."

Susan strokes her cheek gently. "It's OK now baby," she says.

"I did touch it, though."

"Don't worry about it now," Susan says.

———

Carlton's car is a bird-shit green 1971 Buick with a bad muffler, uncertain steering, and a passenger-side window that only rolls up when it feels like it. He's got it jacked up in his driveway this morning, and he's lying face-up under the front end, trying to figure out where the leak is coming from, exactly. The hoses look good; the clamps are tight. If it's coming from anywhere, it's the water-pump, which means he's going to have to do some serious mechanic stuff.

Melody is in the house on Carlton's phone, talking long-distance to Reichler in Moab. They used to be in business together. She says she doesn't love him any more but they still have to work out the company stuff.

Carlton knows he ought to junk the Buick and buy something decent—Japanese or Korean maybe. But he doesn't have enough money, and anyway he's got this weird attachment to the fat car.

Across the street Wesley the madman is mowing his lawn for the third time this week. Carlton has looked out the window and seen him out there at five in the morning working on his sprinklers, painting his front porch, adjusting the ties on his bushes so they'll grow up in the perfect Platonic shapes, like the *idea* of bushes. On his knees filling tiny cracks in the driveway with a putty-knife. Wesley owns every piece of yard equipment knows to Western man—mowers, mulchers, trimmers, clippers, leaf blowers, power rakes. The whole family's full of the same manic energy. Wesley's wife comes to Carlton's door at least twice a month to do good deeds, collect for the Cancer Society, the March of Dimes, United Way, the Republican State Committee, People Against Hunger. They have three overactive children and an enormous dark dog.

It's fairly peaceful under the Buick. Carlton thinks maybe he'll stay where he is for the moment, take a nap, wait for Melody to finish her phone call to Reichler. If he was Wesley the madman, possessed by all that relentless energy, he knows he'd already have the water-pump unbolted and disassembled, lying in pieces on the driveway; he'd be scraping off old gaskets and polishing the reusable parts. The man really is amazing. The whole family's amazing, the way they're constantly doing things to improve themselves, their house, their yard, the world. They go to seminars on self-control, spiritual retreats, marriage encounters. At nights when he's got nothing better to do, Wesley sells Amway products out of the trunk of his car. It's a whole Benjamin Franklin enterprise going on there across the street, and Carlton is afraid of it. It might be American but it's also unnatural.

———

"Mother," Carlton says. He's climbing out of an anxiety dream where he absolutely had to get home now but couldn't fit the ignition key in the Buick. What woke him up was Melody banging on the fender, calling his name.

"*Mother?*" she says.

"Not you," Carlton says.

He slides out from under the car and wipes his hands on a paper towel. "How was Reichler?" he says.

"He wants me back. I told him he could forget it."

"You're still in love with him," Carlton says.

"I don't know what it is, exactly," Melody says. "But it sure isn't love."

"Nostalgie de la boue," Carlton says.

"French intellectuals are assholes," she says. "Why don't you read something American for a change." She goes back inside the house.

———

Reichler wears boots made out of the skins of exotic animals. Today it's ostrich hide, he explains to Carlton.

"Seven hundred dollars," he says. "But they'll last forever if you take good care of them. I know boots."

Carlton isn't sure exactly what they're doing here sitting on his front porch. It isn't the conversation he imagined when Reichler called and said they should talk.

"Buy the best and you'll never be sorry," Reichler says. "Trucks, boots, guns, raingear, it doesn't matter what it is." He puts his feet up on the porch rail, crossed one over the other. The boots, Carlton has to admit, are works of art.

"Women love me," Reichler says, finally getting to the point of why he came. "Always have. It's like they can't help themselves."

He's a small man, compactly built, not particularly good-looking, in Carlton's opinion. He's got a bald spot at the back of his head. What makes women love him?

"They *follow* me," Reichler says. "I don't encourage it, generally, but I turn around and there they are."

"Are we including Melody?" Carlton says.

Reichler holds out his hands palms up, meaning helplessness.

"She doesn't want you," Carlton says.

"She's fighting it a little right now," Reichler says. "But she wants me bad."

On the other side of the street Wesley the madman's wife is washing the family Suburban; she's up on a little stepladder wiping at the car roof with a big yellow cloth. The enormous dog and two of the kids are frolicking on the perfect lawn. Over there it's Norman Rockwell, Carlton thinks. And here on this side of the street we have the kingdom of discontent.

"She'll come back where she belongs," Reichler says. "I just didn't want you to be too disappointed when it happens, that's all."

"What makes you think I'd be disappointed?" Carlton says. "How about *relieved*? How about *ecstatic*? How about who gives a fuck here?"

"Hey," Reichler says.

"Then again she might move in with me," Carlton says. "We'll have kids. Get married. How would you feel about that?"

"Hey," Reichler says.

Across the street the enormous dark dog has grabbed the smallest child by the back of its coveralls and is carrying it around. Wesley's wife has come down off her stepladder and is slapping at the animal with her yellow cloth to make it let go.

"He's just playing with the boy there," Reichler says. "I know dogs."

———

Carlton wakes up in bed half-frozen, cramped and sore from the fetal position he's been in for hours to keep himself warm. When he went to sleep it was spring and now it's winter again. He looks out the window and sees snow everywhere, covering the new leaves, the fresh grass. He reaches for Melody but she isn't there. She hasn't been there for a week. They had the big fight driving down State Street and she jumped out of his car at the stoplight. He figures she's home in bed right now, keeping warm with Reichler, who, she told him once, is a great lay. "He knows women," was what she said to Carlton. "He can do things."

Carlton can do things too, but apparently not the right things. He's never fucked Melody under the tanned skin of a grizzly bear, like Reichler. Or by the light of the full moon in the national park, under Delicate Arch, with coyotes yipping in the background.

"I envy Reichler," is what he says later in the day to Susan and Eileen. The Village Inn is packed with sleazy businessmen eating patty melts and drinking root beer, but nobody's listening, he can talk safely here.

"Envy him what, exactly?" Susan says. Her tattoo is not healing right and she's got it covered with a white gauze bandage, on which she's written *TATTOO* in bold black Gothic letters with a magic marker.

"His boots," Eileen says. She's working her way seriously through a Santa Fe

Omelette gunky with yellow cheese and speckled with red peppers. She stops long enough to pat Carlton's hand. "You're being sort of a jerk here," she says.

"Reichler's a perfect male asshole," Susan says.

"Velveeta," Eileen says, poking at the cheese. "I swear to God this is Velveeta."

"Send it back," Susan says.

"I happen to love Velveeta," Eileen says.

"Reichler does have great taste in boots," Susan says. "But it stops right there."

"Carlton's feeling deprived," Eileen says. "What we should do is take him out and get him a tattoo."

"A butterfly," Susan says. "It would make the guy at the tattoo parlor happy. I never saw anybody who wanted so bad to do a butterfly."

"We want to make your life a better occasion," Eileen says.

———

Sometimes Carlton thinks he'd rather live someplace else than Salt Lake City. Marin County, maybe, or El Paso. Or any place where a majority of his neighbors wouldn't believe in a New York nineteenth century farmer's kid who convinced people he'd read golden plates by the spiritual light of a magic stone in his hat. White salamanders. Indians who are really the lost tribes of Israel. Gods more plural than the Greeks dreamed of. Wesley the madman believes all this and a lot more.

Other times Carlton thinks maybe he'll convert, marry a sweet submissive coed from Brigham Young University, raise himself a whole batch of docile children, buy a dog and a minivan and a snowmobile. He could go to church every Sunday with the madman and his wife and sing weird hymns.

When Melody calls the only thing he thinks he can do is yip into the telephone like a coyote and hang up.

She calls again five minutes later. "Would you like to explain that?" she says.

"I'm lonely," Carlton says. "I'm pissed off about it too."

"Want me to come over?"

Carlton can hear twangy music in the background, some kind of sloppy country-western melancholy, the sort of thing Reichler listens to. "Are you home?" he says. "You're not home, are you?"

"No."

"This is not exactly perfect," Carlton says.

Carlton goes to church with Wesley the madman and his wife. He eats
the diced Wonderbread and drinks the water out of the little pleated paper
cup. He'd forgotten that people used to dress like this, with all the gender
distinctions carefully preserved. Afterwards Wesley treats everybody to
Kentucky Fried at the original location down on State Street.

When Carlton gets home Melody's sitting on the front porch. She's pulling
strands of hair around to the front of her face one by one, checking the ends for
splits. It's something she does when she's bored or doesn't like being where she is.

"I thought you were living with Reichler," he says.

"He's an asshole," she says. "I started to put up a poster and he had a fit
because I was making thumbtack holes in his new sheet-rock."

"Did you ever wonder why they call it that?" Carlton says. "It sounds dumb.
Sheet-rock. Cheap crap glued between two pieces of paper, is what it is. There's
something wrong with America."

"Besides I got tired of all the messages on his answering machine from
women who couldn't live without him," she says. "One of them used to call
from Wyoming and sing into the phone. *Hunk of Burning Love. I Want to Be
your Teddy Bear.*"

"Yeah?" Carlton says. Melody's still doing this thing with the split ends, not
looking at him.

"She did have a great voice," she says. "Kind of a cross between Bonnie Raitt
and Emmy Lou Harris."

They sit like that for a while without saying anything. Carlton imagines
an answering machine singing *Heartbreak Hotel.* Across the street he can see
Wesley the madman's red white and blue tulips that spell out GOD BLESS USA.
The snow just made them grow faster. *Le silence de ces espaces infinis m'effraie,* he
thinks.

"Marry me," he says. "We'll have kids. I'll buy a lawn mower. Maybe put in
sprinklers."

They go inside to the bedroom that used to be an old back porch before
Carlton rebuilt it, reframed the walls, put in double-glazed wood windows.
Sheet-rock. After they make love they watch the black-and-white version of
Invasion of the Body Snatchers on the UHF channel. Carlton hates the scene
when Kevin McCarthy wakes up and Dana Wynter speaks to him in that flat

emotionless voice that lets him know she's been taken over by the pod-people. It makes Carlton so sad he wants to get on his hands and knees right now and howl like a dog.

IN THE SEWERS
OF SALT LAKE

BABY, BABY, BABY

"Let's taste each other's bodies now without pleasure," Martha says.

The living room is full of dogs—she has three, I have four. They have no names; we just call them all "dog" and they never fail to understand which one we mean. It's early evening and the young men from the gas company are lined up in the street outside singing a Jerry Lee Lewis medley. They've got the grand piano strapped on the back of a flatbed truck parked under the maple trees. They sing like fallen angels. *Breathless. Great Balls of Fire. Hang up my Rock'n Roll Shoes.*

"Touch me here," Martha says. "Touch me there now."

High School Confidential. There's a Whole Lot of Shakin' Goin' On. They're all castrati, of course, with those thin pure high voices that specify otherness and absence.

"Baby, baby, baby," Martha says.

I accuse her of bad faith. "You were the one who said without pleasure."

"It came over me like a big wind," Martha apologizes.

She looks skeletal without her clothes on. Ribs like an anatomy lesson. God I love her, but what can I do? This morning I made *fajitas* and she picked out all the bits of chicken, sailed her tortillas like Frisbees to the grateful dogs. Toyed with a piece of green pepper, satisfied herself with slivers of onion.

Tomorrow afternoon it's supposed to be the Utah Power and Light people doing Janis Joplin. Big women in meter-reader uniforms singing the blues.

On the far side of the room, under the moiling dogs the twins are playing. One says "Mama." The other answers "Mama. Mama."

GUSTAVE FLAUBERT

Martha is reading *L'Education Sentimentale* aloud to me by the wavering light of a candle. "'Frederic!'" she says. "'Madame Arnoux!' Frederic!'"

The utility people came yesterday in their gray and green uniforms with the silver skull and crossbones on the collars, and shut off the electricity, the water, the heat. We're lying on the floor under the dogs. The twins are crawling around inside their sleeping bag, two moveable bumps, whining softly.

Martha looks up from the book. "We are folds in the consciousness of our time," she says. "Any other way of looking at it is petit-bourgeois sentimentality."

"Read," I say.

"How can we believe in realism and the novel any more?" she asks me.

"Read," I tell her.

THE ASTONISHING POSSIBILITY OF LOVE

The dogs have dug a complicated system of tunnels in the back yard. They hide during the day in the cool underground dark, and pop up at unpredictable intervals like small hairy Viet Cong. This morning the twins disappeared in the labyrinth and Martha put on her camouflage fatigues and went down after them. It's been three hours now, and I'm still waiting for her to return. There's a light rain falling all over Utah; the state is damp and almost uninhabitable. Martha took the rechargeable flashlight, and a box of Ritz in case she had to stay past lunchtime. Mishka and Mishka, the twins, have always loved to explore dark places; I'm sure they'll be all right. What could happen to them down there under the back yard? The dogs will look after them until Martha arrives with her flashlight and crackers. I'm not worried.

To pass the time I dial the 900 number for women's secret confessions. I'm surprised to hear my first ex-wife's voice, made mysterious and foreign by the long-distance connection.

"I had an affair with the telephone repairman," she says. "He was small ugly dark and Greek. He sang Frank Sinatra ballads in my ear while we made love under the kitchen table. The best part of his body was his feet. They were hairy all over, and so very soft."

I look out the window and see Martha coming out of the tunnel entrance under the gooseberry bushes. She's crawling on all fours, carrying Mishka in her teeth by the back of his overalls.

"Where's Mishka?" I say.

"The dogs are bringing him up," she says. "Do you know they've carved out little rooms down there, with tiny beds and candlesticks made out of empty C-ration cans? It's quite comfortable and warm, not at all what I expected."

THE FRACTAL EDGE OF THE EDGE, WHICH RESEMBLES ONLY ITSELF

My sister calls from Fairbanks, where it's the middle of the night and cold enough, she says, to make the tires on her car go flat before morning. The molecules move too slowly to keep up the necessary pressure, she says. She asks me if I can remember the name of the dog I had when I was a child.

"Charmante," I tell her.

Our sentences cut across each other, thrown out of kilter by the time it takes her voice to travel up to the satellite and bounce back down the imponderable geodesics of space to me. A quarter of a second at the speed of light.

"Charmante?" she says.

"We didn't have electricity in those days," I say. "Or running water. It was during the war and we had to make do with small pleasures."

"Isn't there any way I could make it up to you?" my sister says.

"I've got four dogs now, seven if you count Martha's, but it isn't the same," I say.

"It never could be the same," my sister says.

THE SEWERS OF SALT LAKE

At the entrance, which is in the basement of the county courthouse, a sign forbids the public to pick up anything they might find and take it home. The corporation guides wear their dress uniforms, but instead of the billed caps they have on miners' helmets with powerful carbide lamps. Martha carries Mishka in a sling, tucked against her belly; I carry Mishka in a backpack.

"Mama," Mishka says.

"Mama, mama," the other Mishka answers. Not even Martha knows which is which. In fact the question makes no sense, since they are exactly identical.

The compulsory guided tour is given once a year to citizens chosen by lot from the voter registration rolls. We are happy to be here, though we wish they had allowed us to leave the babies at home. Martha reads to me from her leaflet:

"Various nocturnal animals may be encountered in the tunnels and must be on no account be fed or petted or disturbed in any manner. Remember at all times that you are walking through an environment of extreme ecological fragility."

The guides walk close to us, with night-sticks drawn in case we become unruly or recalcitrant. The one nearest to Martha is very young; his uniform is too big and he seems ashamed of his military appearance. He frowns when Martha stumbles, and pushes her back in line, but not unkindly.

The chief guide holds up his hand to bring us to a halt. We are in the Baptist Catacombs, under what is now Sears and Roebuck. Luminous skulls are set in niches all along the walls, staring at us from the holes which once were their eyes. Loose pieces of dead Baptists have fallen from their resting places and are scattered underfoot. The small finger bones crack like twigs when we step on them.

We arrive under the Temple in time to experience from beneath the ritual emptying of the baptismal fonts. The rush of holy water howling through the golden pipes startles the twins and they begin to cry until Martha gives them suck, one on each breast.

A crocodile drifts softly down the stream only a few feet away, eyes and nostrils barely above the dark waters. A woman in a calico dress throws him a slice of Wonderbread and the guards strike her down savagely with their sticks. Softly at first, but with increasing fervor, we sing old Eric Clapton songs. *After Midnight. Layla. Bell-bottom Blues.*

SOMEBODY'S ANGEL CHILD

FROST'S LOVER HAS A JOB at the University Hospital. For fifty dollars an hour Cynthia lets medical students practice pelvic examinations on the body which, she tells Frost, she detaches herself from for just as long as it takes the young men to get done with their clumsy explorations. She learned the technique from Madame Seroka, her astral flight instructor at the YWCA.

"It's not Cynthia they're poking their hands into," she tells Frost.

"I hate it when you talk about yourself in the third person," he says.

She pays no attention. "You imagine a little hole behind your left ear," she says.

Sunshine comes through the crystals she's hung on the bedroom window. It paints her body with pure wavelengths. She's a rainbow, an abstraction.

"You push down on the soles of your feet from the inside," she says. "Pretty soon you slide right out and you're like floating above yourself. It's a postmodern experience."

On the thirteen-inch Sony cradled above the bed Geraldo is introducing this morning's panel of experts. A woman in her thirties with a beautiful Audrey Hepburn face. *Amanda Scheffler. Virgin.*

"Finish this sentence," Frost says. He props himself on one elbow. "Shuffle off—"

"This mortal coil?"

"To Buffalo," he says. "You always get it wrong."

Cynthia reaches under the sheet to touch him in a delicate place. "All we've got here is a little post-coital anxiety," she says. "Nothing to worry about."

A new face on the screen. *Ed Hostetler. Hasn't had sex in fourteen years.*

"That's medieval," Cynthia says. She stares at the man in the three-piece suit sitting next to Amanda Scheffler. "Next thing it'll be the Black Plague, or little monks walking in line whipping themselves."

"Doesn't he look like Charlton Heston?" Frost says.

"Madame Seroka says Utah might be the new Eden," Cynthia tells Frost. "She says Moab is the center of the fourth dimension."

"Is it too early to send out for pizza?" Frost says.

"Fourteen years without sex," Cynthia says. "Isn't that the most amazing thing you ever heard of? Madame Seroka says the fourth dimension is the dimension of love."

"Hawaiian," Frost says. "I'm in the mood for fish and fruit. Pineapples. Anchovies."

"It might be good, actually," she says. "No sex, I mean. Think of the *energy* you'd work up. That's probably how they built all those cathedrals, right? God told them they couldn't get it off or they'd go to hell, so they had all this *power*, like, left over for carrying stones and carving those little weird statues on the roof. What did they call them?"

"Gargoyles," Frost says.

"Ugly little things," she says. "They don't look religious at all."

"When I think about somebody else touching your body," Frost says. "I go crazy."

———

Down in the basement of the same hospital where Cynthia is right this moment upstairs giving herself to science and education, Frost works with the artificial hearts. He sweeps up, washes glassware, keeps an eye on the gauges which aren't really gauges but icons of gauges displayed on the computer monitors. Two yearling calves have been implanted with the latest air-driven, battery-powered, semi-portable model. The man who invented all this is back East somewhere—Indiana, Pennsylvania—Frost isn't sure exactly, making money and getting famous. He divorced his first wife and married the world's smartest woman. She has a weekly column in *Parade* magazine, where she answers questions about life, higher mathematics, the sex habits of invertebrates, fractal geometry.

The calves don't look like they're in pain, but Frost feels like a Nazi anyway. The beasts are going to die and he's an accomplice. Sometimes when none of the scientists are in the room, Frost tells jokes to the animals.

Lucky, the one in the left stall, isn't doing well today. His head is hanging down and he's not taking an interest in Frost sweeping the floor. A sign on the wall says that it's strictly forbidden to touch the animals, but Frost reaches through the bars and scratches Lucky between the eyes, where there's nothing but skin and a little hair between his fingers and the flat hard bone of the skull. Lucky doesn't even acknowledge the touch. The artificial heart makes a steady liquid humming sound like a dishwasher on rinse cycle.

"How do you make love to a fat woman?" Frost says.

In another hour Orloff and the others will arrive to take the notes and read the instruments. Orloff is the surgeon in charge of the project. He loves college football, owns season tickets to the Utes, wears red and white on game days. He played linebacker for the Georgia Bulldogs before he went to medical school. On bad nights Frost lies in bed in the dark, dreaming up ways to kill him.

"A Frenchman and an American are standing on a streetcorner in New York," Frost says to Lucky. "An enormous limousine rolls by; in the back seat they can see a fat man wearing a three-piece suit, smoking a cigar and drinking champagne."

"I hear something downstairs," Cynthia says.

It's three o'clock in the morning and Frost is having one of his artificial-heart dreams, where the animals can talk. Lucky was telling him it wasn't anybody's fault things were the way they were.

By the time Frost heaves himself up out of the dream Cynthia's gone back to sleep and whatever might have been going on downstairs has ceased. Maybe she was having a dream of her own. About once a month she wakes up convinced she's heard a knock on the front door, or somebody calling out her name in the night. Frost understands that dreams, whatever else they might be, are basically unreliable.

There's a fat full moon hanging outside the window, above the mountains. He could wake up Cynthia and they might make love—she likes sex in the middle of the night, outside the civilized sequence of things, without the usual daytime hang-ups about what's decent and what's not allowed.

He goes downstairs to the kitchen, makes himself a cup of instant decaf and sits on the living room couch next to the dog. Layla lifts her head and opens her eyes long enough to see it's only Frost on one of his middle of the night rambles, then she snorts and goes back to sleep. Frost flips through the TV channels until he finds a show about the strange life that thrives around volcanic springs in certain Pacific depths. Translucent worms sixteen feet long. Animals that look like plants. Plants that look like rocks. He's staring at the unfettered expression of unnamable desires. Unmentionable urges.

He looks over at the dog. She's having a dream of her own; her paws are walking in the air, she's growling, her nose twitches.

When Frost turns back to the TV he's not all that surprised to see Jesus standing in his living room, in front of the screen, blocking the submarine landscape. Frost knows it's Jesus because of the holes in his hands and feet dripping blood on the carpet, and the beatific expression.

"I had this idea maybe we needed to talk," Jesus says.

"Want to sit on the couch?" Frost says. "I'll make the dog move."

"Let her sleep," Jesus says. He sinks to the floor, naturally as anything, ends up in the lotus position. Frost can see all the way through the nail holes in his feet.

"This life," Jesus says.

"My life?"

"It isn't much, is it?" Jesus says.

"I'm having a little trouble getting my head around the whole thing," Frost says. "I'll admit that."

"You've got guilt," Jesus says. "You've got unhappiness."

"Everybody's got those."

"Don't tell me everybody," Jesus says. "We're talking about *you* here."

"What am I supposed to do?" Frost says. "I mean do you have some, like, specific advice or did you come by just to make me feel like a jerk?"

"Well that's a tough one," Jesus says. Behind him the giant translucent worms are writhing obscenely in the warm waters at the bottom of the Pacific. *Who could have thought up things like that?* Frost thinks, watching them loop back on themselves, performing intricate multi-dimensional sex acts. *What an imagination!* Jesus looks down at his feet, pokes a finger experimentally all the way through one of the nail holes, wiggles it.

"Doesn't hurt, actually," he says.

"Preternatural freedom from anguish," Frost says.

Jesus nods. "Preternatural innocence, too," he tells Frost. "I've got all of that stuff."

"Yeah," Frost says, "but what should I *do?*"

"That's the big question, isn't it?" Jesus says. He looks sad and sleepy, not angry about anything.

———

In the meat aisle at Smith's, Frost stares at the steaks in their sanitary plastic wrappings. He has to admit they look terrific. London Broil. Rib Eye. Porterhouse. Sirloin.

"It's all part of the great chain of being," Cynthia says. She reaches over his shoulder and picks out a New York cut. "With Worcestershire sauce and some fried onions," she says. "Mmm!"

A couple next to them is hesitating between chicken breasts with bones or without. The man is older, the woman young and pretty. They're holding hands. "I like it when you touch me," the woman says.

Love, Frost thinks. He and Cynthia buy bananas, oranges, paper towels, green olives, garbanzo beans, toothpaste.

"I need a Magic Mushroom," Frost says. "The living room smells like dog all the time."

"The Cheyenne Indians ate dogs," Cynthia says. "When Lewis and Clark came back from Oregon they used to ask the hotels in Washington to cook puppies for them. Developed a taste for it out there."

"That's disgusting beyond belief," Frost says.

The shopping cart has one sticky wheel and he has to push it crabwise to get it to go where he wants.

"if you're pure in spirit you can eat anything," Cynthia says. "Potato chips. Horsemeat. Rabbits. Dogs."

"People?" Frost says.

She thinks it over. "You'd have to be *really* pure in spirit," she says.

He stops the cart at the air-fresheners. Stick-ups, Magic Mushrooms, things shaped like scallop shells, dwarfs, little animals. "Remember Air-wick?" he says.

"That looked like what it was." He picks up a tiny elephant made of some stuff that feels like soap, holds it to Cynthia's nose.

"Smells like vanilla," she says.

"Where will it all end?" Frost says.

On the way home in the car she sits as far away from him as she can, all the way against the door. He tells her about Jesus.

"You sure it wasn't Elvis?" she says.

"Well he didn't do any miracles," Frost says. He reaches for her but she crouches closer to the door, hugging herself tight.

"Is something wrong?" Frost says.

"I'm not sure I love you any more," she says.

Frost wants to ask her when this happened—everything seemed all right this morning—but when he tries them out in his head the words sound weirdly political.

He tries out alternatives but it all comes down to the same thing. Some questions can't be asked without descending into the rhetoric of stupidity and self-sorrow.

He doesn't see the dog running out from between two parked trucks until it's right under the wheels. Frost stops the car. They get out and stare down at the wounded animal.

"You killed it," Cynthia says.

"It's still breathing," Frost says.

She doesn't answer. Her eyes are closed, her face peaceful in the high beams, and Frost realizes she's tuning out, pushing on the inside of the soles of her feet, concentrating on the little spiritual hole behind her left ear. If he doesn't do something quick she's going to float away and leave him here with a hideously mutilated dog and the vacant body of his girlfriend.

He slaps her and she opens her eyes. "Don't talk to me about love," she says

"Help me," Frost says. "Help me. Help me." He picks up the dog; wet and bloody organs are hanging loose but he pushes it all into the back seat.

At the Holy Cross emergency room they look at him like he's crazy. "We don't do dogs," the nurse says.

"Help me," Frost says. "Please help me."

———

Frost tells Orloff about Jesus. He doesn't mention the nail holes or preternatural innocence. The way he tells it, it could have been a dream.

Orloff walks around the lab with his stiff-legged self-conscious jock's walk, heel and toe, hips barely moving. He bends down to look at a monitor, taps the screen with his fingernail as if wishing could change the numbers, frowns at Frost.

"Dying," he says.

"We're to blame," Frost says.

"You're the man who sweeps the floor," Orloff says. "Blame doesn't come into it."

"I don't like pain," Frost says.

Orloff walks back to the monitor, stares into the screen. "Stop it," he says. "You're not complicated enough to be melancholy."

That night Frost comes to the lab with a U-Haul truck. He leads Lucky out of his cage and down the hallways. Cynthia follows, pushing a shopping cart they borrowed from Smith's Food King. In it is the apparatus that drives the heart. Two lines of clear tubing filled with dark blood trail from the calf back to her.

"Just look at us," she says. "It's a procession."

"We're doing the right thing," Frost tells her.

"*Worse* than medieval," she says. "All we need is to be beating on each other's backs with little whips to make it perfect. They could do us in stained glass."

"Keep up with me or you'll pull out the tubes," Frost says.

They get Lucky up the ramp and into the back of the truck without too much trouble. The shopping cart gets lashed to the wall next to two car batteries Frost picked up at K-Mart so he could keep the heart powered up for the long drive. They're getting ready to go when a hospital security guard comes over to have a look. He's not much more than a kid, with sideburns and a little moustache. He peers inside the truck; Frost takes his hospital ID out of his wallet and shows it.

"Yeah," the guard says, "but what are you doing?"

"Taking it out to the Proving Grounds," Frost tells him. "Government thing, you know what I'm saying."

"Secret stuff," the guard says.

Cynthia leans out of the cab. Her face is a little sullen, but in the weird light from the parking lot she's beautiful. "Are we going or what?"

"Who's she?" the guard says.

"You don't want to know," Frost tells him. It's the first thing he can think of, a line from cheap movies, but the guard has been watching the same late-night shows and helps Frost push the ramp back underneath the truck and lock it in place.

"Should I log this?" he says.

Frost thinks about it, then shakes his head no.

"Got you," the guard says. He gives Cynthia a little military salute and waves the truck out of the parking lot.

"Henry Kissinger, Richard Nixon, the French ambassador, Zbigniew Brezhinsky and a hippie are in this airplane," Frost says. "Suddenly the engines shut down and the pilot comes back to tell them he's out of fuel—there's nothing he can do, they're going down in the middle of Kansas. Worst thing is, there's six people on board and only five parachutes."

The dome light is on, bright enough to show Lucky lying down, clearly not feeling well. The heart is humming along, hooked up to the K-Mart batteries; blood's pumping through the little clear tubes, but Frost can see that the calf is sick, maybe dying. They've been driving for about three hours; they're half-way to Moab. Frost rolls up the back door about six inches and peers out; to the East there's a band of pale orange sky, outlining mountains shaped like the line of a bad EKG.

When he closes the door and turns around he sees Jesus sitting next to the calf, holding its head in his lap, stroking it behind the ears.

"What exactly did we have in mind here?" Jesus says.

"I thought maybe it could die in a meadow," Frost says. "Someplace pretty, with a little grass, maybe a stream. You know."

"That's nice," Jesus says. He looks tired, perhaps a bit depressed, like things haven't been going too well lately. "A little weird, maybe, but nice."

"I'm into kindness," Frost says. "I'd like to be a vegetarian, but it's not easy"

Jesus nods. He looks like he's going to fall asleep.

"We take turns cooking," Frost says. "When it's her turn she likes meat. It's not her fault. She's strange, but she's a good person."

He waits for an answer, an explanation, but Jesus has his eyes closed. Above the mechanical noise of the electrical heart and the humming of the truck tires, Frost can hear him snoring gently. Lucky is asleep too, or maybe already dead, his head in the lap of the man with the holes in his hands and feet, who does, Frost has to admit it, look something like Elvis, or maybe John Kennedy. But what difference does that make, really? By morning they'll be in Moab, the center of the fourth dimension. They'll be looking for a pretty place in the shadow of the LaSalle Mountains. Grass, a stream, maybe a waterfall, some cottonwoods, a place on the earth made holy by the sweet indifferent lightness of love.

FRANÇOIS CAMOIN lives in Salt Lake City and teaches creative writing at the University of Utah. His previous publications include *The End of The World is Los Angeles*, which won the AWP award for fiction, and *Why Men Are Afraid of Women*, winner of the Flannery O'Connor award. He was born in France, and came to the United States in 1951.